*Doody Newman shines in this true to life "Fantasy". – N.Y. Daily Mews*

*Take a bite of cheese and soar into Doody's Adventure. – Chicago Fun Times*

*Say cheese, then smile. – Boston Scratching Mews*

*It's in the whiskers y'all. – Houston Catronicle*

*Be careful which suitcase you hide in. – Skin Mom's Magazine*

*When is the last time you hugged your pet? – Catanooga Times*

*This book will make you bright eyed and bushy-tailed. – The Dog Catronicle*

*Snuggle up with dog bones and treats. – Miami Barking Dog Press*

*Watch out for the paw prints.*
*– Pawtucket Mews*

*The book is the best non-electronic*
*entertainment you can find.*
*– Tailahassi Post*

*"Jack, Jo and Cooper...*
*Keep your tails down please".*
*– Atlanta Taily World*

*Snuggle up with warm milk and treats.*
*– The Kansas City Paws*

*Say "cheese" and fly.*
*– St. Louis Post n Scratch*

*Doody Newman loves this book.*
*– New Jersey Cheezy Mews*

*You'll wanna to take a cat nap after*
*reading this "Fantasy". – The Whiskers Globe*

*This book is a must for cat, gecko, firefly,*
*dog and children lovers. – The Furry Gazette*

*Take off on this First Adventure with*
*Doody Newman. – The Catnip Express*

# THE CATTAILS OF DOODY NEWMAN

## THE ADVENTURES OF THE BROWNEST TABBY IN TEXAS

# BARBRA BALLINGOFF MCGEE

### ILLUSTRATED BY
## ALEXANDRA MONTEMAYOR

The Master COMMUNICATOR'S WRITING SERVICES

# DEDICATION

This book is dedicated to my mother, Patti. You not only gave me life but you gave me the necessary tools to make it through my life with ease. If I had only followed instructions completely, I would have breezed through. We both know that was not God's plan for me. You taught me about respect and honesty, and that I am never alone in this world. When things don't go as planned, there is always a silver lining, a reason why, and another plan right around the corner. My life journey so far has been amazing, and I am so grateful for the beautiful relationship we have and that you have been there for all of it. You are my mother, my best friend, my mentor, and the woman I have always wanted to be when I grow up. You inspire and encourage me to do and be anything I set my mind to. You believe I can, then I believe I can, and then I do.

You have always been my superhero.

I wish everyone had a Patti in their life because she sure makes my world a lot brighter. I love you mom, Babes.

# TABLE of CONTENTS

# ACKNOWLEDGEMENTS

I want to first thank God, because, without my faith in him, none of this would have been possible. I also want to thank Michael who listened to every new chapter that came out of my head and never appeared bored or uninterested. Thank you for telling me not to sweat the small stuff and for all that you do for me every day of our beautiful lives together.

I want to thank Sharon for taking my hand and leading me down this literary journey we are on, and never leaving me alone for a minute. Our chance meeting was a gift from God.

Thank you to my sweet Beth, you always help me find the solution to my problem

I want to thank my fellow "Miracle Angels" for all of their support every day and especially

since I started writing this story, I'm so grateful you all were put in my life, I'm never alone.

Thank you, Alexandra for bringing the character "Doody Newman" to life. Your talent and creativity are as amazing as your sunny personality

Thank you, Hilary, for editing my creation, without losing my voice or the message, you were definitely the right one

And finally, If I could, I would like to thank my fur babies, the actual animals that inspired this story. They will never know how much they have taught me about life, just by living theirs. If you don't have a pet in your life, and you are able to rescue a cat or dog, I would highly recommend it, because it will change your life, and theirs. It changed mine.

Check out the local animal shelters in your area for more information.

# PROLOGUE

Today was the absolute worst day to fly. The fog had gotten so thick you could slice it with a knife. The road was barely visible as I drove to the airport. I passed quite a few cars on the shoulder waiting for help and I was running so late I had to park in the airport terminal. *That's gonna cost me some money, but it's worth it to be on time,* I thought. I nearly forgot my bag in the car as I jumped out in a frenzy and headed to the terminal. Then I was dodging people and hurrying through the concourse trying to look as much like a professional as possible, when I saw some of my flight crew and slowed down to join them. We continued our walk to the gate and I felt proud beside my fellow crew members, all of us sporting crisp uniforms with our matching luggage trailing behind. We turned the corner to find our airplane, parked at the gate, waiting just for us.

We are the crew for flight 1945 to Seattle today. As flight attendants, we are responsible for everyone's comfort and safety, while the pilots are responsible for properly flying the airplane, the passengers and crew to the destination (preferably on time.)

I still get excited to fly. Like a child waiting in line over and over to board the biggest roller coaster, it never gets old.

The jetway was attached to the front of our airplane, but the fog was slowing down our departure. Our massive craft poked its nose through the mist, looking like someone had gone crazy and sprayed whipped cream all over the windshield. We headed through the waiting area, thick with travelers, to check in with the gate agent, but before we reached him, a flurry of activity caught my attention.

A strikingly handsome man sat beside a small animal carrier, and it appeared the inhabitant didn't seem too happy. I walked over to offer my assistance and to introduce myself (after all, he was *super* handsome.) The man looked down into the carrier at his feet, and I could tell from his red face and the way he fidgeted, that he was embarrassed at the ruckus coming from the crate.

As I bent down to peek inside, I asked, "Oooooooh, who do you have traveling with you today?"

He looked at me, his face pink and said, "A very unhappy kitten, I guess."

By then, I was on my knees peering beyond the grid door of the carrier, trying to lock eyes with a darling cat who hunkered inside. "Oh, what a beautiful little kitty," I said. "How old is he and is he yours?"

"No," He answered, quickly. "He belongs to a friend."

When I looked up at this frustrated stranger, I cooed, "I just love, love, love animals. I have a few cats at home, as well as a couple of dogs. Oh! If I had more room at my house, I would take him home with me. He is so sweeettt."

He regarded me with a strange *yes, you are very nice, but a little crazy* expression, before telling me, "I made a promise to my good friend, Jay, who works at *Paws for a Cause* that I would fly this kitten to his new home today. Otherwise, I would consider letting you have him, but that promise also involves a few special people who are waiting for this little guy in Seattle, and I like to keep my

word. He'd been pretty quiet up till now, but all of a sudden, he started hissing and meowing at the top of his lungs..." The man paused, and I waited for him to finish. "Actually," he said, "it was about the time you came over to talk to me."

"He probably smells my fur babies on me. They like to slide past me on my way out the door to leave their scent, that way I can take them with me wherever I go." I chuckled, just thinking about it.

The carrier started moving all over the place again. Quite a commotion was going on in there. Kitten howls grew louder and louder. I started to slowly back away.

"I would love to have a good look at him, when he calms down," I said.

The kitten-escort replied, "I promise to let you see him when I get situated in my seat on the plane."

I told him I couldn't wait as I turned to go, then proclaimed, "Kitties are so sweet, especially when they're babies. Everything on their bodies is so teeny tiny."

I waved goodbye and hurried toward the gate agent, had my ID checked, then hustled down the jetway, calling back over my shoulder, "I just love, love, love animals!"

The crew members, who had been waiting for me, all echoed in unison, "WE KNOW!"

Then we all rounded the corner of the jetway and disappeared from view. The gate door clicked as it closed behind us.

The rest of the crew and I chattered and laughed as we put our bags away. I was the last to throw my bag in the overhead compartment, and for some reason was hit with a strange feeling like I had forgotten something. I paused, did a mental checklist of the contents I had packed earlier that morning, but didn't think I had left anything behind. So, I dismissed the hunch as nothing to worry about and got back to work, swinging the black nylon roller board up and pushing it into the bin. The noise it made when it finally landed sounded like "PLLLOOOOP!" A few seconds later the overhead door slammed.

All this racket was not unusual for an airline crew's daily routine. The happy gabbing of the crew, the unique sounds that were all a part of prepping the plane, the baggage ploopping... it's all familiar chaos we hear all the time. But today, I would find out, was going to become anything but routine. Today was going to be quite extraordinary. In fact, nobody knew it yet, but today would change history. Particularly for one brown tabby. Yes, today was the day we would get to witness a new face, a new hero, that we would hear a new message. Today, we were preparing to meet Doody Newman, and our lives would never be the same...

"PLOOOPPP"

*Hey, what was that? Huh? Shhh...wait... What the heck? yawn... I was just having the best dream! There was a field and the sun and cheese—wait, where am I? What's all that noise? ...And what's under my whiskers? I feel a little confined, a little squished, if you will... Wait, I can't get up. I seem to be stuck. I can't move my arms or legs—what happened? Oh, my good feline, OH MEOWWW, I think I made a terrible mistake! It was an error in judgment or maybe I've been so off my balance I didn't even pay attention or notice what was going on around me until it was too late. Maybe I've been so tired and upset about my future that I passed out not knowing where I was laying my whiskers... It's muffled and loud—and there's a hiss or a sound like wind and it's so noisy it's making the voices faint. I feel like I'm in some sort of container, and it's not a cat crate, because I can't see outside and besides, it wouldn't be so tight in here. Maybe I'm stuffed inside a box or a suitcase?*

*Oh, my good feline, I think that's what it is! I must have fallen asleep on my skin-mom's freshly washed clothes. They were so warm and smelled so heavenly I couldn't resist. Now I think I'm stuck and I don't even know where I'm stuck...and OMG...could I be with my skin-mom at work, and if that's so... I'm in real trouble! She's a flight attendant (the coolest job EVER!), which means she leaves the house a few times a month. My skin-mom flies in the biggest airplanes in the universe, and is responsible for the safety and comfort of people from all over the world. I'm afraid if I'm really stuck inside her suitcase, inside an airplane (or worse, in the belly of the airplane), I may be here forever! If that's true, it means I'm headed somewhere way far away from Texas and my adopted siblings, and my HOME.*

*How could this have happened? I haven't been myself this past month, so I guess anything's possible. But this? Trapped in a suitcase on an airplane, possibly in the air, waaayyy far from the ground. Oooh, I'm so scared, I wish Uncle Blackie were here, or the Orange Gecko, or even the fireflies...*

*Wow, OK, what should I do? What would Uncle Blackie do? What would I do if I were thinking straight? Maybe I should leave a note. Yes, I KNOW*

*I'm a cat, but I'm a very special cat, if you ask me. I can do things most humans can't even do, so writing a note is not a big deal. But who would read it? I found a piece of cheese inside this bag. I just ate it and my whiskers should be getting longer any minute—the cheese helps my special powers, which involves my whiskers, but more on that later...if there is a "later." ...I need to find a pen... OK, here we go. Ooooh, here's a flashlight, too! No, it's not a flashlight, it's my skin-mom's extra iPhone! I think I remember how to work it! I could call home and... No, what am I thinking? Who am I gonna call? And nobody would understand me anyway! I'm a cat! The skins don't understand felinglish. So, I'm gonna have to leave a note, maybe record one! No, the language barrier again... Alright, I'm gonna type a note! Now that my whiskers have grown (remember the special power thing I mentioned), I have lots of toes to use to text speedy fast... Here goes...*

"To whom it may concern, or anyone who reads this... If I don't make it back, please let someone, anyone, know... My name is Doody Newman. I am a brown tabby cat, the brownest tabby in Texas. I have two moms. My first mom is my real mom and she has fur. My other mom has skin. I was born in my skin-mom's apartment in the year 2000. But we now live in a big house in Houston, Texas with my fur-mom, Wiggy Lynn and her twin brother, Uncle Blackie. I also have five adopted brothers and sisters. Prissy Ann, Rustaford James, Mini Me, Azreal (Lil' Girl), and Xander. Against my better wishes there are three dogs, too. Jack (the big hound), Jojo (the silky one), and Cooper (the bulldog). We have an awesome loving family, all the food we want, lots of toys to play with, and lots of treats. I love to play with my cat siblings and gobble treats, but more than anything, I LOVE cheese and wet food, to chase lasers, geckos, and frogs, and guard the house. My favorite thing to do is fight crime (by crime, I mean anything I see that I would consider illegal, like being mean for no reason, bullying, or just downright bad stuff.) If I see it, I'm gonna do something about it. Nobody knows this, but I have special powers... I can... Oh, scratch all that! Just tell somebody, anybody, I'm missing, AGAIN!"

## How it Started

Every story should have a beginning. Well, this is mine. I was just an average cat until I was gifted with magical powers. It all started when I was playing outside in the backyard one summer night just before midnight. The night showed the fullest moon I had ever seen. I was hanging in the grass chasing lizards and frogs when I came upon a gecko. He was bright orange, and in the light of the moon, looked like his scales were changing colors from purple to blue to lime green. He didn't run when he saw me and stood on his hind legs, like I do when I'm trying to reach a treat.

I leapt over into his direction and said, "Hi, I'm gonna chase you until I catch you and then let you go, so I can chase you again."

He narrowed his eyes at me and said, "If you let me go, I can show you things you would never believe existed."

I was stunned, as I had never talked to a gecko before. They had always been too scared or too busy running from me. But I was a little curious, so I said, "OK, whatcha got?"

The Orange Gecko said he had magical powers and he would share them with me, but only if I didn't tell anyone. It would have to be our secret. When I agreed, he said, "Meet me tomorrow night at this same time, in this same spot and I'll show you."

I cocked my head back at him and asked, "Are you sure this isn't just a trick so you won't get chased?" Then he promised me it wasn't a trick, as he pointed his finger in the air. A bright light flashed and a huge rainbow of a million colors shot out from his finger and went for what seemed like a thousand miles. I agreed, and this time without any doubt and with my eyes wide open. By then, my skin-mommy was calling us in for the night and I left him in the yard as I headed toward my house, but I dreamed about that rainbow all night long!

The next day, all I could think of as I played and slept and ate and slept some more and then groomed my brown fur, was the bright Orange Gecko and the rainbow. It was so hard to contain my excitement, but I had to keep the secret because that was our agreement. Finally, the night came. I went out to play and wait for him. As soon as I'd started thinking about what was to happen, I sensed someone standing behind me.

When I turned around, there he was—the bright Orange Gecko—standing taller than I remembered. His orange glow was so vibrant, it lit up the whole corner of the backyard. On either side of him were two fireflies.

He looked at me and said, "Are you ready?"

"Yup!!!" I meowed.

He smiled a little, then said, "OK, here we goooooooo!" As soon as the words had left his lips, the fireflies shot into the air and did loop-de-loops then came back down and hovered right next to me on either side of my body. They joined their little firefly wings together in front of me and asked me to put my right paw on top of them. As I did, the Orange Gecko wrapped his tail around and around the fireflies and my right paw. An amazing thing happened after that! He got bigger and bigger and started changing colors right before my eyes! Lime green, purple, pink, blue, yellow—so many colors at once! I saw a flash of dazzling light and then felt myself lifting into the air. All around me was the rainbow, just like I had seen the night before. But this time, I was IN it! So many beautiful colors were everywhere at once! Green and yellow and red and blue and gold and pink and purple! I had never seen anything so awesome!!! I felt warm and safe and cozy.

As I was floating in the rainbow, I heard an angelic voice whisper in my ear..."Doody Newman... You are a very special kitty. You will do great things and help many animals and people. You are so very loved and you will never be lonely. You have been chosen..." I didn't know who was talking, but it was the most beautiful voice I'd ever heard, it sounded a lot like my skin-mommy's voice, if you can believe it.

Suddenly, I felt a pounce on my back... I woke up to see I was sleeping on the bed and the sunlight was shining on me through the window. My adopted sister, Prissy, was trying to wake me up because she had heard a can of wet food opening.

I tried to shake the sleepy feeling, but I couldn't focus. Had I dreamed everything that had happened last night? Had I imagined it all? I didn't know, but my stomach had started grumbling, so I jumped down to go get some grub...

# Prissy

Let me tell you about my adopted sister, Prissy. We're about the same age. My skin-mommy brought her home when I was close to three months old. She once told me she is a day older than me, but we look a lot alike, 'cept she is a silver tabby with a red nose, and I'm the brownest tabby in Texas with a brown nose, if you ask me. She likes to get me in trouble and I always seem to follow her around. She is kinda bossy, since she is a day older than me, and I just have to do as she asks because she is so beautiful. Plus, we've been together the longest and she is my best friend. We do everything together and very rarely separate. I love her. So, when she pounced on me that morning, I got right up and went to eat.

I couldn't stop thinking about the night before—had it really happened? Had I dreamed it? Am I'm going crazy? It was all too much for me. I went outside to look for the Orange Gecko but couldn't find him anywhere. I even went to the place where I'd last seen him, but no luck. I did notice that I had a funny feeling in my tummy whenever I walked over to that spot where all the lights and rainbow stuff had happened. And I sat there for what felt like hours, just watching all my adopted brothers and sisters playing in the backyard. The funniest thing was that nobody noticed me, even though I was sitting right there in the yard. I yelled to my brother Rustaford, but he seemed to ignore me... *Humpf, that wasn't nice.* I tried yelling to my fur-mom, still no response. I was starting to get tired since I'd already been up for a whole hour (us kitties need lotsa sleep), so I decided to take a nap. I'd worry about everyone ignoring me later.

I woke up from my nap with a jolt. The dogs were barking at something in the yard... I got up and went to check it out. When I walked out the back cat door I noticed all three dogs yelling their heads off in the corner of the yard, in the same place I had seen the Orange Gecko, the rainbow, and fireflies. I wondered what it would be like to see through a dog's eyes. I know they can see stuff I can't. I wished I could talk to them and ask, but

I don't speak dog. I slinked back toward the rear corner of the yard to see what they were barking at. That's when it happened—the dogs couldn't see me! I thought this was unusual because most of the time when they see me they chase me. This time? I walked right past their noses! They looked like they thought they smelled something, but didn't seem to see me.

Could I be *invisible*?

Does this mean I really had met the Orange Gecko and the fireflies and that I had *actually floated* inside the rainbow? I was determined to find out if I was invisible. So, I walked right up to the big dog, Jack, stood in his face and said,

"Hey, you, big dog, your breath is so bad, it could stop traffic!"

As soon as I'd said it, I turned away super fast and squeezed my eyes shut, because even if he hadn't understood what I'd said, I was still in his face and veeerryy close, so surely, he was gonna get me for that one... *Nothing? Really?* I tried it again, but louder...

"HEY, YOU, BIG DUMB *DUMMY*, YOUR BREATH IS SO BAD IT MAKES THE FLOWERS WILT!"

*Still nothing?* ...I wasn't sure how to take all this, but maybe something really had gone on last night with the Orange Gecko. I was extremely curious now, wondering if he and the fireflies had

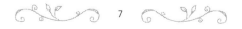

made me invisible. If so, when had it happened and when would I go back to being me again? Would I ever get noticed and would my fur-mom know where I was? Would my best friend, Prissy, miss me and would I ever be able to lick my skin-mom's beautiful soft face ever again?

Wow, I am sad. I think I'll go inside and look for some wet food, maybe my skin-mom got my favorite tuna with shrimp gravy. That will make me feel better... Then I'm gonna take a nap, all this thinking and wondering and excitement has made me tired. I keep thinking... *Never mind, I'm too tired to think. I'm gonna go take a snooze.... No! I'm so weirded out about this.... But I'm so tired...*

I knew it was really strange none of the dogs, especially big dog, Jack, had seen me. It was crazy odd, and I just kept thinking about what I saw. *What did I see*? I can't explain what it was. Maybe it was another cat? No, it was a bird. No, it was like a shadow, my shadow...but not exactly a shadow. Because to cast a shadow, you need to be a solid form, and if I'm not visible, if I'm not noticeable... If, in fact, I am invisible, how could I possibly cast a shadow on the fence? But the shadow didn't move like I was moving. It moved opposite of me, like it was looking at me, waiting for my next move, like it was watching me...

Oooooh weird! I got goose bumps under my brown fur as I thought about the something I thought I might have seen—that was or was not seeing me at the same time. Even if nobody else can see me, everything had made me SOOOOO tired... *I promise I'm going in for my nap now.*

# 3

## No Reaction

I told you about Prissy, and I mentioned my mom, Wig and Jack, the biggest dog, who is a yellow lab and ridgeback mix. Lemme tell you about some of the others I share this big house with in Houston, Texas. I have two orange tabby brothers, Rustaford and Mini Me. Mini for short. I have a really, *really* big, white, thick-furred younger brother, Xander, who wears a gray toupee. There's Uncle Blackie, of course, who looks exactly like my fur-mom with swirls of black, silver, gold, and white, except for the white shark-tooth-looking mark on his face. I also have a beautiful, classy littlest sister, Azreal. She is a Siamese snow leopard blend with the bluest eyes I have ever seen. We call her Lil' Girl. Then, there are two other dogs who share the house with us,

Jojo, a black lab and border collie mix and Cooper, a bulldog. Cooper is new to us, only a year old, but I already like him—and I know he will be able to help me in future escapades.

The last time I left off, I was in the backyard yelling at big dog, Jack with no response. I didn't understand why he couldn't see me. I didn't feel any different, I didn't notice that I look any different, although I haven't looked in the mirror today. But, let me go over the most recent events anyway.

So, I slept, got up and ate, groomed myself, slept again, chased a few geckos in the backyard—yuck, it was like 1,000 degrees out. Then I went inside to take a nap again after I'd noticed it was already 8:00 A.M. I did realize no one had spoken to me today, and when I tried to talk to Rustaford, he ignored me. The real test would be when I tried to talk to Prissy. If she ignored me, then I would know for sure something was definitely wrong. I slinked over to where Prissy was sleeping. (She always grabs the best spot in the house and has quite the nap schedule). First, she lies in my skin-mom's dresser thingy. It has two doors that open from the middle, and shelves lined with soft clothes. I think she puts them in there just for us. The dresser is just the right height for me to jump into, but Prissy gets the first shift anyway, on account of she is a day older than me and all. When Prissy is finished with the first shift, she jumps down and goes to eat. After grooming and checking out the play going on in the gen pop (that's what we call the rest of the house), she gets tired and takes her second nap in the clothes bin, which is usually lined with fresh warm clothes that smell like the sweetest flower I've ever sniffed.

The clothes bin is one of my favorite spots because when I get up, my brown fur smells sweet like my skin-mommy, and that is the best smell in the whole world! For her third nap of the day, Prissy heads to the master bedroom, to snooze on the biggest and best bed in the universe. (That bed is so comfy! It moves up and down and jiggles and feels *incredible* on my toes). Before she gets up on the bed, though, Prissy has to stop in the master bathroom to get a drink of water, not from the bowl that all of us are forced to share, but from the elegant fountain that stands tall in the middle of the room.

All she does is nudge my skin-mom's arm and my skin-mom will get up and adjust the fountain for her! Wow, I still have to ask her how she does that, because it makes her look even cooler and more graceful than any cat pretty much in the world. So anyway, my plan was to pounce on Prissy just before she jumped on the fountain, and say, "Heeeyyyy yooouuuu...whatcha doin'??"

Then she would pretend I hadn't scared her as she licked her right paw and said outta the corner of her mouth, "Nuttin."

I had the plan down and was ready to pounce, and I started to shake my butt and tail to get the energy to do it, too. But that's when I noticed the shadow-looking thing again. The weirdest part was that I saw it for real in the mirror this time! I actually saw eyes...real eyes, looking at me. *Oh, my good feline, my own shadow is looking directly at me!*

I didn't have the time to spend obsessing about the shadow, because I had a pouncing date with Prissy, so I jumped as high as I could and landed right in front of her face! Then I got this close, and said, "HEY, YOUUUUU, WHATCHA DOING?"

But no paw licking and no talking and no nuttin happened. That's when I knew without a doubt, that Houston, we REALLY, REALLY did have a problem.

## Pow Pow Pow

Even though my Uncle Blackie rarely speaks, my fur-mom and her twin couldn't be more opposite. They were both born on my skin-mom's porch in August, 1999. From the time they took their first breath, my fur-mom hasn't stopped talking. I don't know where she gets all her words. If I stayed up for a million hours for days and days and days, I wouldn't even know half the words she knows.

My Uncle Blackie is the coolest dude I know; he never really makes sounds, but you know what he's saying by the faces he makes. Like, he will point his eyes in one direction while everyone is talking about going out to play, and you know he means "Let's go!" Or when a can of wet food is opened and he wants some, he'll just walk over to it and my skin-mom will slide it into his dish. Or when the big dog, Jack, or Jojo, the silky one, are all bark, bark, barking at him, and he simply stands there and looks at them, not making a peep. Like I said, Uncle Blackie—coolest dude I know. I love my Uncle Blackie, that goes without saying. Whenever I need advice or a whisker to lean on, he is always there to help me out. Once I figured out the big dog, Jack hadn't been able to see me and the experiment with Prissy hadn't gone the way I'd planned, I thought I'd try one last thing, to know once and for all, if in fact, I was truly the brownest (and now the most invisible) tabby in Texas.

My plan was to get my Uncle Blackie to see me, or at least to sense me. He likes to hang out on the front porch, and I'm not allowed out there, so I had to catch him before he left. I knew he would be on the cat buffet table eating wet food at his usual time, so before he finished up and headed outside, I was gonna dip my paw directly into the food, so he'd get some clue I was around. And OK, I know it's only been 24 hours, but still, I can't believe nobody has noticed I'm missing— I'm pretty important in this house, if you ask me!

I waited by the kitchen and watched everyone eating and playing and grooming. Meanwhile, I was plotting my move.

The plan was to get to Uncle Blackie before he went out front. He was just about finished with his wet food. (I know when he is done because he pukes it all back up again, and big dog, Jack gobbles it). Jack was hanging around because he knew he was going to get some hot nuggets soon, so the time would be right to make my move. I slinked over to the big table where the cat buffet is and jumped quietly onto the chair, then slooooowly sneaked onto the tabletop where Uncle Blackie was eating. I stood in front of him and didn't say a word. Just stuck my paw into the food he was eating. It smelled yummy, like tuna steak with shrimp gravy, my favorite! It's Uncle Blackie's, too, because it makes for one great big gob on the table, and because it's easier on his throat, on the way up, with the gravy—it slides right out. Hmmm... Maybe that's why he doesn't talk much, because he's afraid he's going to hurl anytime he opens his mouth.

So, I was watching and waiting, and waiting and watching. (Boy, he doesn't stop to breathe)! I was bobbing and weaving and going from side to side, and finally, I got a second to punch my paw out and into the food. I used my right paw for good luck, since that was the one the bright Orange Gecko had asked me to use. Hopefully, it would work and Uncle Blackie would be able to see me. Then I'd be back in sight for everyone to lay eyes on, and I'd see all my siblings as I pounced with Prissy. I'd see my fur-mom and kiss my skin-mommy 's face again.

*Here goes nothing*! I squeezed my eyes shut and jammed my paw into the wet, gooey fish-smelling gravy. POW, POW, POW! I opened my eyes to see wet food, shrimp-gravy, tuna chunks, and shrimp legs everywhere. Oops, I guess I got too excited and punched too hard. I slowly looked up at Uncle Blackie's face and all I could see were two green eyes blinking; he was covered from the top of his black ears to the tip of his groovy tail in the best-smelling, slimiest fishy goo this side of Texas, if you ask me.

He just stared at me—*AT* me—*can he see me? Did I have a breakthrough? Is my life going to go back to normal again?* I opened my big mouth in the smallest way and squeaked out, "Can you see me?"

The voice that came out was like nothing I had ever heard come out of this brown tabby's throat; I sounded like a mouse and made barely any noise at all. *What the heck was that?* I'd finally gotten my chance to once and for all, talk to the one feline that may be able to see me, and that was all I could come up with? I tried again.

"UN-CLE BLACK-IE, can you see me?"

*Wow... What is wrong with me?* I NEVER have trouble talking, or yelling, or being seen.

That gecko must have really done me in. OK, one last time. I opened my mouth and it seemed like my throat turned into the longest tunnel ever, with echoes and crickets and was that the ocean?

"UNCLE BLACKIE, CAN YOU SEEEEEE ME?" There. It was out. He looked me right in the eye and said, "...Gecko."

# 5

## Docar

The night before I met the gecko, a bizarre thing happened to me. Not that the next night wasn't strange, but the night before was the strangest thing that had happened to me—I mean, before the Orange Gecko and the fireflies and the rainbow came into my life. It was during the midnight crazies. I walked down the hallway and saw what looked like my shadow on the wall. I turned to check it out and it did the opposite of what I did, like it was looking at me as I was looking at it. I ran up and down the stairs a few times to see if I could lose it, but no luck. The shadow moved with me. Then I sat down, but the shadow didn't, it stayed standing. I wasn't staring at it, but when I turned around it was still standing. I was a little afraid, and a little interested at the same time.

So, I turned to it and asked, "Who are you?"

It was silent.

I asked again, "Who are you and what do you want?"

Again silence

I wondered what the thing could be. I'd always thought it was a part of me since my shadow stayed with me everywhere I went. It seemed to feed on my fear, because I noticed when I got scared, it grew bigger, taller, and a little wider. One time, it even grew as high as the ceiling. I started to feel uncomfortable, as this brown tabby had never seen anything like it before... I couldn't understand what it was and if it really was not a part of me, then where had my original shadow gone? The situation had gotten so far out of hand, that I decided to scat, so I flew down the stairs and ran into the master bedroom as fast as I could. As I slid under the bed, I smacked right into Xander.

He was sleeping, so when I bumped into him and knocked his toupee to the side, he woke up with a jolt, sat up and fixed his faux hair hat, and asked what was the matter. I was breathing so hard, and my heart was beating so loud, you could hear it all over the house. I told him what I had seen, and his face turned even whiter than it already was. The toupee he'd just fixed fell to the side again.

That's when he told me a story he had heard a long time ago, when he was living on the street. Once, a group of street cats would sit around the fire and spin yarns (as they put it.)

Xander sat up, as he said this was not a story to tell lying down. But the tale he shared next was the strangest story this brown tabby has ever heard.

A long time ago, there lived a big tomcat named Docar. He was savagely bad, not just breaking-the-rules kinda bad, like, I hate to even think of it, *evil*. He didn't like anyone, and nobody liked him. He was a loner who had lived on the streets his whole life, and always tried to make the girl cats cry. The tomcats, well, he had a point to prove to them, and would start a fight any chance he could. If there was a tough tomcat new to the area, Docar wanted to set the record straight that he was the biggest and baddest cat in the neighborhood. He worked his way across town fighting every tom from every block. And he won every fight because he made sure of it; he would not give up until the cat he was scrapping with either gave up or he won.

As the story goes, there was a fog that came through the town that lasted for three days and three nights. The fog wasn't the normal smoke-gray-looking color. It was more of a dark charcoal. You couldn't see anything in front of you. Just like when it gets pitch black outside at night. Except this continued for 72 hours straight. Preventing anyone from seeing anything anywhere. It made the air hard to breathe, and it was so thick it produced a rain-like effect on everything outside. The storytellers say it was the eeriest looking three days anyone had ever seen.

Docar was not scared. He walked around for three days and nights looking for some tomcat to fight, but nobody would go outside in the strange phenomena. He walked and called to anyone who would listen, but nobody budged. The whole city fell silent due to the unusual weather. On the second day, as he was turning into an alley, he heard a low growly and ghastly voice, say, "Docar, you are the baddest and most feared cat in all the city, are you not?"

Docar stood tall and answered, "Yes, you have heard of me, and you are absolutely right!"

Then the voice said, "How would you like to be famous as well as feared, and never worry about losing a fight for the rest of your nine lives? And how would you like to triple your lives to 27 lives?"

"Well," Docar said, "that is a very tempting offer. What if I say yes? I would like to have all of that, so what would I have to do? And by the way, how do I even know you are telling the truth?"

"SILENCE!" The voice yelled so loudly the ground shook. Docar was not afraid. He was never scared of anything. He lived his life with such a dislike of all things that he had nothing to lose, so nothing ever scared him or disrupted anything he ever did. The voice said it had been watching him, and that it thought he would be a great candidate for what he wanted. Well, Docar had never had anyone compliment him on anything before, and he felt a twinge of...delight.

"So," Docar said, "go on."

The voice said, "It's been two days and two nights, and on the third day this fog, actually called 'foag,' will lift and you will have everything you ever wanted, anything you will ever need. You will never lose a fight, and you will live 27 lives. At the end of that time, I will tell you what you will need to do for me to keep up your end of the bargain."

Docar thought about it for a minute, and said, "Why do I have to wait all that time for you to tell me what I need to do?"

And the voice said only three words.

"You will see."

Docar thought about it, and it seemed like a sweet deal. Even if he had to lose a fight or give something up, it wouldn't be until he'd lived out his 27 lives, and he would probably be ready to give up by then...whatever he had to...so he agreed. By that time, it was almost morning and he was tired. He found a tire in the alley and went to sleep.

When he woke up, he felt different—stronger, with more energy, and not as hungry as he usually was after getting up from a nap. He made his morning rounds of bullying the local cats as he strolled. Noticing, as he walked, that not only was the fog (or foag) gone, but he had a sort of fog (or foag) following him wherever he went. He knew about shadows and how the sun cast them when you stood in its rays. But this shadow was different. It made a sort-of hissing sound when he walked, and whoever he approached looked like they were petrified before he'd even gotten to them. Docar was thinking that part was really cool, that it was even better that his foag hissed and was heard before he'd even arrived.

After that day, Docar's life was never the same. He was even more feared by everybody around him than he had been before. He noticed the more fights he won, and the more famous he became, he didn't have to eat as much. It felt like he had just eaten every time he fought. When he won, he usually felt so full that he would have to take a nap to sleep it off.

After a while, there were no more local cats to fight, so he decided to take it on the road. He went from Washington state to Maine, from New Jersey to California, from Florida to Texas and all the states in-between. As you can guess, Texas was so big, both tall and wide, and the felines, well, let's just say, everything is bigger in Texas. Docar liked Texas so much he decided to stay. About halfway through his journey he noticed that he'd stopped eating altogether. He didn't need food anymore, because the evil feeling that he got from fighting and winning was filling him up in ways that no mere can of sardines ever could. He also noticed the shadow that followed him everywhere *was* everywhere now and had somehow become a part of him—that it *was* him. In fact, it was more him than he had ever been. It was around life 24 that he started to get tired and bored of his "new" life, and when he wanted to go to the big wet can in the sky. But he had made a promise that he would continue on until he had lived 27 lives. He became the most famous and feared cat in all the nation. But even with all the fame and fortune and everything he'd ever wanted or needed, he was not happy. He still wanted more. He would often say there's got to be something more to this life. But sadly, he would never find that something more. Because eventually, he became less cat and more foag. Near the end of his

life, he didn't even have to walk anymore; he just floated. That mysterious substance that interested him and covered the land those three days early in his first life eventually took him over and became something that was once called Docar, the most famous and feared cat ever. Docar was no more; he just became one with the fog, or so they thought...

His whole life, Docar had wondered, "What will I have to do to become the most famous and feared cat in the world?" On the last day of the last life of the most famous and feared cat in the nation, Docar finally found out what he was to do. The voice that had remained with him every day and throughout every life, spoke again at the end, and this voice sounded tired and faint.

"Docar," the voice said, "you have been given everything that you could ever want, or need, and now it is your time to give back. You will roam this earth as the foag you have become. You will influence the evil, bully the innocent, and feed on the fear of the chosen and the good."

With that, the voice was gone.

The greed and dislike of all things good made Docar choose to live a life that looked like it was the envy of everyone. In the beginning, it had really been great, but after a while, his life as he became more and more one with the foag, got boring... When he finally learned what he was to do forever, he had purpose again. He was to roam the earth for all eternity, spreading bad to all who would listen, to those who thought like him, and who wanted what he wanted. He would feed on the fear of the chosen and the good. Wherever someone had a doubt about doing good, he would arrive and make sure the good had been erased from their minds and replaced with fear and evil instead. When he finally understood he would be miserable forever, he decided if that were so, he would be the best at it; he would make sure to prey on the weak, to bring misery and doom to anyone he could.

When Xander finished telling the story, I felt a lump the size of a golf ball in my throat. My stomach had butterflies going 'round and 'round, and my nose had started doing the "twitch."

*Oh, my good feline, could my very own shadow be the Docar foag?*

## Rustaford

My brother, Rustaford, has always been orange; he was actually the very first orange tabby in our house, but he hasn't always been a loner. He was left by some family who didn't want him anymore, didn't need him, or maybe they got new furniture and he didn't match the color anymore. Or maybe they went to live in a place that didn't allow pets...

*HOW CAN YOU NOT ALLOW PETS?* Who makes these rules? I mean, who doesn't like pets? What are you? Evil, cruel, and friendless, and you wanna make the whole planet hate you by buying a building and fixing it up so everyone wants to live there, and then when you rope them into moving in, you spring on the people that you don't ALLOW pets? I'm telling you some people are just plain mean, and I wouldn't want to live there any-way. Don't they know that petting fur makes you feel better? I guess they don't, because they will never ever in a million years feel better, since they don't want, have, nor will they ever get pets...if you ask me. How sad, but it makes me mad; it gets me going. So, what? Maybe once in a while, we throw up on the carpet... Or maybe we have an accident on the floor and someone slips on it and falls on their behind. Or maybe we get so excited and just have to run around and around and claw the couch and sprint up the curtains. What's wrong with that? OK, now where was I? Oh yeah, Rustaford.

According to him, he was a hobo living on the hardened streets of modern Texas suburbia, working for every morsel of food he ate and then some. He had to chase his own geckos and mice and anything he could catch just to have some company while he scrounged for crumbs. He al-ways says, "When you've been out on the streets as long as I have, you'll eat anything." And he sure does. So, Rustaford told me, he was out gathering food, when one day, he noticed some-body had moved into the newly-built house at the end of the ravine. He had watched as the build-ers had come by day after day and made what looked like a massive cat carrier, only way taller. They worked day and night, and at the end of every day, left lots of crumbs and chips and soda cans and wrappers that all made noise when you pounced on them.

He watched as the humans started moving things into the big cat carrier. Day after day, more and more stuff was brought to this place by truck and car. Finally, all the activity stopped and he went to check out what was going on. That's when he noticed a few cats in the windows, and thought he heard a dog barking, too. He continued to watch the house, and after a few weeks, decided to make his move. He said he figured if there were cats living there already, that the humans with them clearly must've liked animals. He thought if he behaved and didn't make a mess maybe they would like him, too. Maybe they would even let him stay.

One day, he walked right up to the window where one of the humans was and said, "Hey, do you think you have any room for one more weary kitty? I've been walking the streets for years and I'm lonely and tired, and I want to live with a loving family I can call my own. I want to have lots of brothers and sisters to play with and all the food I can eat at any time."

Since humans don't speak cat, it probably sounded more like "MMMMMEEEEEEEEEEEEEE OOOOOOOOOWWWWWWOOOOOOOWW-WWW," if you ask me.

He told me after he'd spilled his guts like that, he walked away, because he wanted them to really want him. He thought if he walked away after telling them what he wished for, it would make him seem more likable. If he started out small and gave bits and pieces of himself instead of all of himself at once, maybe the humans would like it better, because what if they didn't want any more cats? And what if he wasn't ready to give up his freedom after all? Even though he'd seen cats in the window, he hadn't noticed any felines outside, which meant these were INDOOR CATS. After being outside for so much of his life, Rustaford wasn't 100 percent sure if living inside was the life for him. He also had a few other houses lined up that he was checking out, "'Cause, you know," he'd said, "Just 'cause a human family wants you, doesn't always mean you are ready to give up your freedom to live the life they have planned for you. You have to be entirely prepared to sacrifice all your freedoms. No scrounging for food anymore, no pouncing and playing anytime day or night, no eating whatever you want, anytime you want." And then he went on, "But when I really thought about it, giving up my freedom meant I wouldn't ever have to go hungry again. I would have all the food and treats in the world. I would have toys and brothers and sisters to play with. There would be heat in the winter, air conditioning in the summer, and soft beds and warm places to rest my whiskers. The very best part of it all would be the human hands petting my fur, scratching under my chin where I can never reach, humans to kiss my head and love me forever and ever...aaahhh." Whenever he tells the story, at this part, he always just shakes his head and says, "Where was I?"

He went back a few more times to those humans, then eventually let them catch him (although I don't think he ran all that fast, if you ask me.) He joined us in the house we all live in now, and it was love at first sight. Between Rustaford and Prissy, not Rustaford and ME. I mean, I love my brother Rustaford, but I don't LOVE love him...yuck. He would chase her all over the house, hiding around the corner or on the other side of the door, and when she would pass, he would pounce, pounce, pounce. He would be the first in line for treats and get two so he could give her one. He sang her love songs, wrote poems, and drew hearts in the wet food, but still she wouldn't pay any attention to him. After a time, he gave up, a little...but I think he still loves her.

After Prissy broke his heart, Rustaford and I became great friends. We would get the midnight crazies and tear up the house. Once, we were zooming around the corner during a midnight run when he ran right into a door. It knocked him out, and I sat with him and stared at his face until he woke up. After that, it was he and I, game on; best buds and the youngest boy felines in the house. I was so glad to have a brother, because before that my fur-mom and Prissy would nag me if I didn't do what the girls asked, and you know how girls can be (real catty, if you ask me.) *Ahh, Rustaford, I miss talking to you, I miss talking to everybody. Sniff, I think I'll take a nap.*

I woke up from my nap, and you know when you are still half asleep and you start thinking about all the stuff that goes 'round and 'round in your head? You know, that part just above your whiskers and in-between your ears... Well I got to thinking; the morning after the night of the fullest moon I had ever seen, when the brightest Orange Gecko and the fireflies came to me and I had floated in the rainbow and heard the angelic voice, Prissy had woken me up. She'd pounced on me and said she'd heard a can of wet food opening. *If she couldn't hear me when I yelled, yelled, yelled in her face, a few inches from her red nose; if she couldn't sense I was there even after I'd seen her whiskers move when I'd opened my big mouth and let out a whoosh of breathy air that smelled like the best tuna with shrimp-gravy this side of Texas. If she really couldn't see me, how come she'd pounced on me that morning?*

I also got to thinking about my shadow that kept showing up at all times of the day and night. I mean, I didn't ask it to be there. I didn't invite that weird-acting look-a-like to follow me around everywhere, and it was getting a little annoying that he kept showing up. I need to try to talk to him again the next time I see him. He kinda has a creepy vibe to him, like he isn't there for a party, but more for a meeting, a serious one that may not end well for me. I get goose bumps under my brown fur every time he is around. Boy, in just two days my life had certainly changed—my once simple and uneventful reality, except for a few rumbles with my siblings, had now been filled with surprises at every corner and scratching post.

# Uncle Blackie and the Big Fight

The last time we left off, I was on the buffet table with Uncle Blackie after the pow-pow-pow, losing my voice, and covering him with the tuna chunks and shrimp-gravy. OK, so remember, he looked right AT me and said, "... Gecko," after I had made a bunch of silly noises that were meant to be words. Well, I had finally gotten out what I'd wanted to say, but it could have sounded angry. Anyway, it doesn't matter because he'd looked directly into my eyes and said a word. Saying anything is a big deal for him on account of him not talking much. But he'd said, "GECKO!" Wow, when he decides to say a word, any word, he really makes it count.

I tried talking to him again. "Uncle Blackie, you can really see me! Did you hear me, or see

me, or both? Or did you just say gecko because you saw one or smelled one, or heard someone else say the word, or...or...or..."

Just as I was getting the rest of the words out, my very big...no...I mean, my *very* big, thick-furred, younger brother, Xander, came flying out of NOWHERE. He's so fluffy, he can barely jump on the bed anymore, but just then, he came flying onto the cat buffet table, looking like one of those floats you see in the Thanksgiving Day parade. He gracefully glided through the air with his mouth open and his face wobbling and fluttering as the air whooshed through his mouth and filled up his cheeks. I would bet my next treat that the air had kept him up there. As he landed, it was like slow motion and I saw him crash into my Uncle Blackie, so he went flying onto the kitchen floor. They began to wrestle around and around on the ceramic tile, and I couldn't tell who was who. Of course, my Uncle Blackie is black, silver, gold, and white, and Xander is all white 'cept for a few gray splotches on his back. And of course, his gray toupee looked like it was gonna go flying into the dog water every time he got on the top of the furry feline ball of arms, legs, ears, whiskers, and tails flying around all over the kitchen. *C'mon guys, GUYS! Slow down!* Just when I'd thought I was gonna get a chance to get a word in, my other brother, Mini Me, (also an orange tabby), came sliding in like lightning across the floor. He was chasing the ring from the milk jug, which is the best toy on the planet, if you ask me. He tried to stop, but slammed into the fury of fur happening right in front of him instead. I think of Mini Me as one of the heavies in the family, and he did not disappoint me that day. He knocked that fur ball into the dog buffet and water, wet dog food, dishes, and treats exploded all over the place. Everyone stopped in their tracks then, like time had stood still for one second. After that second, they picked right up where they had left off, rolling around and wrestling. This time, the ball of fur looked like one of those orange creme popsicles with chocolate in the middle. 'Round and 'round, and left and right, and bouncing; every once in a while, one of them would come flying out of the top of the heap and then go back in. Wow, I have never seen anything like it—a fuzzy ball of 12 legs, 3 tails, 6 ears, and about a thousand whiskers all wrapped into one. I yelled and yelled, but nobody stopped. I was getting a little mad, because I wanted to talk to Uncle Blackie and ask him if he knew what was going on. I needed to know why he'd said, "...Gecko." If it had been because he'd seen me or heard me. *What the heck was GOING ON?* Just then the ball of fur came to a stop and Xander's gray toupee went spinning off his head

into the dog's water bowl. I guess it's all fun and games until someone loses a wig.

Mini Me was named after the first orange tabby, Rustaford, because he was so small when my skin-mommy took him in that he followed Rustaford everywhere he went. That first year, Mini Me was so scrawny and scared that he needed someone to watch over him and Rustaford took him under his whiskers. He barely spoke to any of us in the beginning, but Rustaford, being so worldly, built up his confidence so much over the years that by the time Mini Me was fully grown, he was a pretty cool dude. No more scrawny orange cat; he grew into a distinguished long-furred cat with piercing green eyes, and the biggest, fattest tail I had ever seen. Lemme just tell you, when he saunters into a room, all the feline ears turn, boys and girls. He has a way of conducting himself so all who encounter him are left in awe.

Of course, no one is perfect—everyone has that one thing that just annoys you. Like me, with people who don't allow pets. Well Mini Me's thing had to do with Xander. When Xander first came to the house, he was very sick, skinny from no food, and he had a broken nose and road rash on his paw pads. He needed lots of 'round the clock care, but then he started to get better, and when he did, he walked around like he was a big shot, pushing all the other cats around. We didn't much like that. Since he was not the oldest, nor an original. The four originals, or the original cats, are what we call the OC's, and they are my fur-mom, Wig, my Uncle Blackie, Prissy, and me. We are like the elders of the house. My fur-mom, Wig is the boss of the bosses; she even tells the dogs what to do, AND they do it! Dumb, dummy dogs...if you ask me.

So, Mini Me has a problem with Xander, and in turn Xander has a problem with Mini Me. Prissy, my beautiful sister, is the most beautiful feline this side of Texas. Lil' Girl is beautiful, too, but in a different, more exotic way. All the male cats that meet Prissy just melt; they fall in love with her on the spot, and Xander and Mini Me were no exception. As soon as Mini Me met her, he fell in love, hard, but Mini Me, being the gentle cat he is, was too afraid to ask her on a date, or profess his love for her. He would just stare at her instead, wishing he had the nerve to make his move. Xander, on the other hand, was big and bad and had no fear, so when he was nursed back to health, he became the suave one, the debonair one who showered her with affection and professed his love over and over. But of course, Prissy, as the true queen she is, would not give him the time of day. All Xander's attempts to woo Mini Me's one true love, broke his poor heart. Xander was aware of Mini Me's love for Prissy, but continued to try to win her heart anyway.

One day, while Xander was sleeping on the landing at the top of the stairs, Mini Me saw his opportunity to reveal the one secret that Xander had been keeping from everyone, especially Prissy.

So, as Xander was comfortably dozing, and by comfortably, I mean, all four legs sprawled out with his head over the edge of the big, fluffy pink pillow at the top of the landing (yeah, I know pink isn't exactly a masculine color, but this bed is the cat's meow, probably the most comfortable and lush cat bed in the whole house.) Anyway, Mini Me snuck up to him and knocked his toupee off. It whipped across the room and landed on a woman my skin-mom was talking to in the living room. This woke Xander up with a jolt, and when he realized what Mini Me had done, he jumped up from his sleep and tackled Mini Me and they started rolling all over the floor. There were bad words, loud growls and high-pitched yowls heard for miles. Prissy came out to see what was going on, saw Xander without his toupee on and a shiny bald spot on the top of his head, and she giggled nervously. Well, he saw the look on her face, then felt beyond embarrassed. This marked the beginning of the longest ongoing battle between Xander and Mini, and all over a girl. That just doesn't make sense. *Girls? Jeez, what a waste of time.*

The point is, Mini and Xander don't get along, and anytime they get the chance to scrapple with each other, they jump on it. The day of the fight of the century was no different, except it was all about me, and the fact that I seemed to be missing, but nobody was noticing, let alone trying to find me. It was just like any other day. I started to think *so this is what it would be like if I were really gone, everyone doing their thing, having fun and going about their business. I don't like it. I truly thought everyone loved me. Guess I was wrong.*

Mini, Xander and Uncle Blackie continued to fly around the room wrestling and yelling and rolling all over the floor and they were concentrating so much on winning that when Xander's gray toupee flew into the dog water, they just stopped for a second. Xander felt his head, realized what had happened, and jumped back in with more force. The fur was flying literally, and the main event had sparked the attention of everyone in the house. Prissy was first on the scene, then my fur-mom, then Lil' Girl, and of course, Rustaford, being the ladies cat he was, was tailing right behind. Even the dogs, Jack, Jojo, and Cooper, were sitting down to watch the show. I looked out the window, and noticed a few strays selling seats, if you can believe that. I think it cost one Temptations treat per tail. I saw the pretty, orange, girl tabby, Ginger, selling catnip in the crowd, too. What an event! The three of them would not be interrupted for a minute, and I could not get a word in, so I guessed I'd have to wait for them to stop. I grabbed a seat like everyone else as well as a piece of cheese and kept my eyes glued on the whirling fur ball. After a while, Uncle Blackie stepped out and his second string went in. I didn't know him, but it didn't surprise me to learn Blackie had a backup; he is without a doubt the coolest cat I know. Xander and Mini kept wrestling on the floor and when the replacement went in, the ball of fur rose into the air like a balloon. While Uncle Blackie stayed on the sidelines, I went over to him to ask him if he could see me.

He looked directly in my eyes and said, "I know what it is that you seek."

I said, "You can see me! How is that possible? Nobody has been able to see me for the last 24 hours, after the Geck—"

And just then I remembered I was supposed to keep the secret I'd promised the Orange Gecko, or I would lose my powers. (That is, if I had any! All I'd noticed in the last day was that nobody could see me, and *what was the sense of having special powers if nobody can see you using them?*) It was all too much excitement for the brownest tabby in Texas, so I went to grab the sleeping spot Prissy usually occupied at that time of day.

When I woke up, I saw Uncle Blackie in the hall, on the way to the front door. I stopped him and looked around; I had finally gotten him alone, then I asked him if he could see me.

He said, "My dearest nephew, you are completely missing the point. It's not whether I can see you or not. Rather, it's about how you are going to use the new found powers you have been blessed with."

*How did he know where I was, and how could he see me, and how in the world did he know I had special powers?* Oh, my good feline, I had so many questions. After I'd stopped thinking in my head, which I do almost every minute of every day, I noticed Uncle Blackie walking off. I stopped him again and asked how he knew where I was and how he knew of my special powers.

"Well, you are my sister's son, my favorite and only nephew. You are very special and very loved, and you deserve to know the truth. You better sit down for it."

We went behind the long couch in the living room; he sat me down and started talking with the most serious face I had ever seen on my Uncle Blackie. What he said next would change everything in my life as I knew it, forever. As he tells it, on the night of the fullest moon I had ever seen,

I was in the backyard chasing geckos and playing. He had been on the other side of the fence prowling around, where I'm not allowed to go. He'd gotten caught in a situation with a family of ducks who had been swimming in the ravine when a duckling's foot had gotten stuck under a rock. This baby could not swim to catch up to the rest of the family. She was crying and crying, but the others couldn't hear her because they were telling jokes, laughing, and talking.

My Uncle Blackie ran down to see what the problem was and the little one said, "Please Mr. Cat, would you help me? I'm scared, and alone, and my foot is stuck under this rock. Please don't eat me. I promise I will repay you somehow."

Blackie, being the kindhearted feline he was, went all the way down to where the baby was and tried to free her foot. He pushed and pulled and wiggled the leg, but no luck. He finally saw a piece of wood and wedged it between the two rocks and freed the baby's foot. But when he did, got stuck himself. The baby duck thanked him and swam off to be with her family, never knowing that Blackie was in trouble. Blackie tried to get loose, but knew without a doubt he was in huge danger. The water was rising, and fast. He pulled and pushed and wiggled his leg, but was unable to free himself. Then he panicked and started meowing and howling as loud as he could, but no help arrived. He remembered thinking, *wow, my house is right there. I can hear Jack and Jojo barking, and the cats playing. I can smell my skin-mommy baking chocolate chip cookies. I'm so close, yet, so far.* Finally, after much struggling and yelling, he accepted his fate and started breathing slowly and trying to relax, so his final breaths would be less painful. The water came up and covered his body and he went into his final slumber. He remembered seeing a bright light just before he closed his eyes for the last time.

A blazing whiteness in the middle of the sky woke him up, and he thought it was the light at end of the alley that he'd always heard the elder cats talk about. The light that cats saw after they passed on, so he knew what had happened. And he was sad at first, but when he looked back on his life, he became grateful he had made it to the age he had. He'd lived a full life filled with great food, great friends, and wonderful skin-parents that had taken care of him every day of his life. He'd gotten to fall in love a few times, to go out catting around anytime he'd wanted and then some. It had been an amazing life... He just hadn't wanted it to end so soon. Just as he was reflecting on his life, he saw the bright light again, followed by a huge rainbow that shot up into the night sky. And it was coming from our backyard. He floated up and over to where the rainbow was,

and said he saw me there, along with the fireflies, and Orange Gecko. He said he was curious to know what was going on, so he got a little
closer, and that's when the bright Orange Gecko
observed him, not in full cat form. He knew my
Uncle Blackie had passed on.

The gecko said to him, "Hey there, my fine
feline, are you transitioning to kitty heaven?"

My Uncle Blackie said he thought so, but
everything just had happened so fast, that he was
confused. See, cats have nine lives, and Uncle
Blackie had lost one of his lives when he'd rescued the duck.

Ordinarily, he would have gone to heaven
and then he would have been transitioned back
to earth. But things can get kind of confusing up
there with all that red tape. In the end, the Orange Gecko decided to bless Uncle Blackie with
a prompt return to earth. It had all happened so
quickly, that Uncle Blackie said he had still been
trying to figure things out.

The Orange Gecko had heard what my Uncle Blackie had done for that baby duck, and how
he had sacrificed his own life to save her. Since
the gecko was already there, anyway, to perform
a special feline power ceremony for me, the Big
Guy told him to find Blackie and expedite his return to earth because of his act of kindness. This

meant my Uncle Blackie had seen the whole ceremony, rainbow, fireflies, and all!

I was flabbergasted that he had seen the whole thing!? I needed to know more. Uncle Blackie said that because he'd died a hero, the gecko had arranged a speedy return to earth for him.

The day I'd woken up on the bed with Prissy pouncing, he'd woken up in the backyard, with his new life, or number two, only he didn't have to go to the interview or do the background check and all. Whatever they do up there. He'd just jumped into his new life, with a new cattitude and a new love for the world.

So...he can see me! *Wow, I feel different. I feel alive, I feel, I feel...* Just then a can of wet food came flying at my head and I had to duck. I'd almost forgotten about the big fur fight going on. Calmly, I had another bite of cheese and sat to watch the tail end. All these new developments had made me tired, I had to go take a nap. I was so tired, I stumbled back behind the couch. The last thing I thought I saw before I closed my eyes was *a...toy...mouse...and some treats ...Zzzzz.*

# Powers

I understand now about my Uncle Blackie being able to see me and all, because I've heard that when cats pass over and come back, they can see things that other cats can't. I think that's the coolest. It makes him even cooler than he was before, so now he is officially, the coolest cool dude that has ever walked the streets of Houston. He is so cool that when he passes by, a whoosh of cool air follows him and when he opens his mouth to speak, ice particles fly around him like a circular spiral, creating an echoooooo that goes on and on.

After I had the talk with my Uncle Blackie, I felt a calming feeling; I guess this is what my skin-mommy calls peace. Whatever that means. I woke up from my nap with a new catittude. Like

I could take on the world...and all it had taken was for someone who loved me to believe in me and trust me. I just wanted to be seen. What's the point in my wonderful life if I can't share it with someone, anyone? I was getting lonely being by myself. I had been so sad for so long, because I'd thought I was invisible (well, I am invisible), but at least Uncle Blackie could see me, and that was enough. I was just about to give up altogether and try to find the Orange Gecko to have him take my powers away...but...wait... *powers? Yes, POWERS! Oh, my good feline...I forgot all about my special powers. I can do whatever I want. I'm invisible AND I have powers, but what kind of powers did he give me? Lemme see, can I make something move? There's a toy mouse under the couch!* I squished my eyes together and ....*Nnnnnnmmmmm alakazam!* I opened them up, and nothing. *OK, so that's not my power. Maybe I can make something explode.* I looked at the mouse again, and *nnnnnnmmmmmmmalacazam!* Nothing. *Hmmm, I'll have to keep trying till I can find what powers I was given.* I saw a treat stuck inside the couch on the side of the cushion; *lemme see if I can make it disappear. Yeah, lemme try that...mmmmnnnnmmmmmm aaallllacazam abracadabra hocus pocus dom...min...ino...cat!*

I heard something...*what was that?* It sounded different. I don't ever think I've heard a sound quite like that before. I opened my eyes and looked in the direction of the treat. It was still there. *But that noise, something had happened... what was it?* I sloowwly started to walk over to where the treat was, and I tripped... I mean, I have been known to slip a time or two during our midnight crazies, but I've gotten right back on my feet within seconds, and I don't think anyone has ever noticed. I am not uncoordinated by any means, if you ask me. So, what could I have tripped over? I didn't see any yarn, or toys, or shoes, or dog toys. I started to walk again, but I was pulled back to where I'd started. *Was I stuck? What in the feline was going on?* I looked both ways and what I saw right then couldn't be happening. There was no way for it to be possible. *What in the heck? Wow, weird, but how, when, what did I do?* It shocked and excited me at the same time. This would be the biggest, best beginning of a new adventure for the brownest tabby in Texas, if you ask me.

## I was Chosen

OK, so I've told you a lot and gotten you to a specific part of the story, but now I want to take a break for a minute and tell you... I may have left some stuff out, because I get so excited sometimes that I forget the small details. If I did, I'll fill y'all in later. It's not easy being the smartest, most graceful, toughest, and most intelligent crime-fighting brownest tabby in Texas. And I haven't gotten the chance to meet the bright Orange Gecko again yet, but hopefully I will in the future. I did have a dream about him, though.

My dreams are usually about running in the biggest field in the world; I don't know where this field is, but who cares, it's AWESOME! I run and run and run. I don't know if I'm chasing something or being chased, and I usually wake myself up because all the running I'm doing in my dream makes my legs go back and forth on the floor, like I'm running in place. I must look super funny, because a few times when I've woken up, my skin-mom has been standing over me ready to take a picture. She does that a lot anyway. I don't know what she does with the pictures. You can't eat them, and they don't make good cat toys, but it makes her smile. That makes this brownest tabby in Texas happy, too

Oh yeah, the Orange Gecko. But before we get to that, I forgot to mention a small, tiny almost-not-even-worth-mentioning detail, but I will anyway.

So, in my dream about the bright Orange Gecko, he comes to me in the rainbow, the same one I floated in the night my whole world changed forever. He was tall and standing on his hind legs, and had the fireflies with him on either side. I like those fireflies; their light never goes out and they are always smiling. They must have a great life. They can always see where they're going, and can light the way for anyone who is without a light. They can also brighten someone's day, (someone who is not having such a good day...kinda like they did with me.) In my dream, the gecko told me I have special powers, that they were a gift, and that I was chosen to change the world from bad to good, luckily only a small piece at a time.

He told me I would have to figure out how to use my powers for good, and never for personal gain. He explained that meant I couldn't use my powers to get something I wanted or like if the dogs were barking too loud or being annoying, I couldn't make their water bowls fly through the air and cover their heads or something like that. I would have to make my world and the world of anyone who needed help—and who asked for that help—a better place. I guess, like carrying a message that everything will be OK, no matter what, and that it will get better...tomorrow is another day, stuff like that. I still don't understand the whole thing, but luckily, I'm pretty smart, and I'll figure it out over time, 'cause I'm the brownest tabby in Texas with the best life any feline could ask for. I am loved and I WAS CHOSEN, and that is a fact, if you ask me.

The real test would be if I could use the powers I had been given for good. It would be nice if I actually could figure out what those powers were. I tried moving an object, and that wasn't it; I tried making something explode, and that wasn't it, and then when I went to MAKE something disappear, it hadn't disappeared. But something else had happened. I didn't know how it happened, but maybe it was what I'd said, or how I'd said it, or what I was thinking at the time, but when I opened my eyes that day after trying to make that treat disappear, what I saw does not make any sense. I've never in my life, heard or seen anything like it. I was stuck in my spot, and I almost tripped when I tried to move, and the thing, or things, that were preventing me from moving were my very own, brownest-tabby-in-Texas, WHISKERS.

That's right, my very own whiskers had grown a thousand times the size they normally were, and they were what had prevented me from cruisin' along. I felt like I was stuck inside a piano, with all the strings, except those strings were attached to my face. MY FACE. I had tripped over my own whiskers, and I don't know if you have ever seen exactly where whiskers come out of a cat's face, but it is in a very tender spot on our cheeks, so when they get pulled, it yanks your whole face, yeeeouuuch. And to have them so long that I'd almost tripped on them, well, it took a while for the pain to go away. Talking about it now is giving me a FFA or a Feline Face Ache, so I'm gonna take a nap. *Oh, huh, what? Wait, is that a can of wet food opening?* I'll be right back, gotta check it out, and then have a nap.

What a beautiful nap I had. I got to sleep in the pink bed, the softest, fluffiest cat bed in the house. It's the one on the landing in the middle of the stairs, and it's put in the exact spot to catch the sun at just the right time of day. As I lie there, it warmed my ears. It's the bed Xander usually sleeps in, and boy does he leave a dent. That cat is so long and heavy, he has stretched out the bed and left a big hole right in the middle, but I was so tired, I barely noticed. I also didn't notice the sun had disappeared behind a bunch of gray clouds. Those gray clouds looked a little like Xander's toupee...*gray toupee*... ...*What cat wears a toupee?* All the felines in this house make me giggle.

The sun was gone. All I could see out of the huge windows that cover the whole wall in the back of the house was bits and pieces of the backyard. I noticed there were lightning bolts coming down from the clouds, and I heard thunder. The big dummy dogs don't like that sound, and they usually hide under the bed or under a table, so it's nice not to have them on my tail for once. In-between all the thunder, I also thought I heard meowing. *Was one of my siblings in trouble or was it someone else?* I got up to get a better view, and still heard the meowing. I walked into the living room, then into the garage, then upstairs, then stood outside the closet door, 'cause sometimes someone gets stuck when my skin-mom leaves the door open and you know how curious we can be. But the meowing didn't get louder, so I didn't think anyone was in there...which meant it was probably coming from outside.

I went outside, and saw the clouds and lightning and heard the thunder, but there was no rain yet, thank goodness. I don't like water, any kind of water. If you ask me, water was meant to go in one end of me and out the other, never to touch this brown tabby fur. I get a little crazy when I feel even a drop of liquid on my purrrfectly brown sheen. It changes the way I look; it turns me into a skinny cat and I don't appear put together, and you know I have an image to maintain. OK, meowing outside, rain, thunder, and lightning. I'm going to check it out. Then all of a sudden, I spied a dark spot about my size. *Hey, what's that? It's that shadow again, and it's on the wall! I don't have time for that shadow now!* I took off in a flash.

I went to the back of the yard, where the Orange Gecko had given me my powers and changed my life, and I heard the meowing again. When I looked through the small lines in the fence, you know the ones that show you what's on the other side, I saw a mama cat with six small—I mean, weensy small—babies. Their eyes were still closed, and their ears were round and close to their heads, which I knew meant they were only a few days old, if that.

She was laying down and the babies were all on top of each other, legs and arms and ears and whiskers, all in one big ball in-between their mama's arms and legs, all cozy and safe. So, where was that meowing coming from? It was getting louder and louder because the thunder was crashing, and I knew (and the vocal chords knew, too) that the rain was gonna come crashing down at any second. If that happened, this brown tabby might get a little uncomfortable. You know, liquid, no like, not good for brown fur.

I continued on to find the owner of those vocal chords; he or she could be an opera singer with the volume coming from that throat. I could have used their help the day I'd tried to talk to Uncle Blackie when nothing would come out of my mouth. I looked in the shed behind the house; nothing. I looked in the bushes near the pool; nothing. I looked in the barbecue pit, and I heard the meow grow louder, so I made myself as small as I could get and slinked under the pit. Inside the pit under the bricks was the smallest, cutest kitten I had ever seen. He reminded me of me as a baby. OK, so remember I'm invisible, AND I have whiskers coming out, but I don't know how to make them work, and I'm in a small spot.

I said to the baby, "Hi, little guy, I see you got separated from your mom and siblings. Are you OK? Are you hurt?"

The baby kitten stopped meowing and look-ed around, with his closed eyes. He couldn't see anything and even if he could have, he wouldn't have been able to see me.

He said in the smallest voice I had ever heard, "I'm so very scared and so very cold. My mommy left with all my siblings to go to higher ground because of the storm, and forgot to get me. Now, I'm stuck under this brick, and I can't see and I'm not strong enough to lift the brick. I'm so sad because I'm never gonna see my mom again and I'm all alone and meeeeeooooowwwwww!"

I told him not to worry or be afraid, and to grab my paw so I could pull him out. He asked who I was, and I told him that his mom had sent me to get him and he believed me. He started to reach his paw out to mine, but just then a loud clap of thunder sounded. I heard a few drops hit, and smelled rain on hot concrete.

He jumped and went back under the brick and started to cry again. I told him I used to be afraid of the rain, too, but every time I had been afraid, I would just think of my fur-mom and how her fur smelled and how warm and cozy she al-ways was, and I wouldn't be afraid anymore. I said to try it, and he did and it seemed like he felt better. I tried to grab him again, and when he went to touch my paw with his paw, it went right through, like it missed. *Darn, I'm invisible, so I'm not able to touch him.* I was trying to think of how to get ahold of him when I remembered my whiskers, but I didn't know what I had done to make them come out long. I tried abracadabra, alakazam, hocus pocus, and a few other words, and then I finally felt a tickle and saw the whiskers go flowing out and grab that little nugget with the round ears and those big vocal chords. My whiskers wrapped around and around his little body until he looked like a mummy, with only his head and flat ears showing. I carried him out of the area he was stuck in and all the way to his mom. She cried real feline tears of joy that she had her baby with her at last, that her family was complete.

She couldn't see me, but said, "Whoever you are, and wherever you are, thank you so much for blessing me with my lost baby. You are a miracle of kindness."

*WOW!* No one had ever thanked me for anything. I'd never even thought about helping those in trouble, but for some reason, I got this feeling in the bottom of my stomach that traveled all the way to my heart, which was already beating out of my chest. That feeling was the best feeling I'd ever had; it was something I'd never felt. Even better, dare I say, than eating my most favorite tuna with shrimp gravy. It was something new and that made me feel like I had found what I was meant to do with my kitty life. I had a purrrpose.

*Oh, thank you, bright Orange Gecko. Oh, thank you, beautiful fireflies. Oh, thank you, Uncle Blackie. Oh, thank you, my most beautiful fur-mom, Prissy, and all my siblings. Oh, thank you, my best skin-mommy in the whole world, for loving me and taking care of me when I was sick, for feeding me, and playing with me. And thank you, everyone I have ever met! I am the happiest kitty on the whole planet, in the whole universe! This is without a doubt, the best day of any day that I have ever lived. This has been the best day of my life, and I can't wait for more. All the things I thought were important in my life become small when I think of how I helped that baby kitten and his mommy. How happy they'd been to be reunited. From this day forward I promise to be the best, brownest tabby in Texas I can be.*

# 10

## Whiskers

After the best thing that has ever happened to me happened (when I rescued the baby kitty and the momma thanked me), I started to think of new things I could do, people who could use my help. It gave me such a great feeling that I couldn't sleep for days. All I could think was if my fur-mom knew and Uncle Blackie knew, too they would be so proud of me. I'm proud of me. What else could I do?

I had been so sad about being invisible that I hadn't even thought about what good I could do for someone else. I guess Uncle Blackie knew something I just didn't understand at the time, which doesn't surprise me because he not only is the coolest dude that ever walked the earth, he is the wisest dude I know. So, I had to figure out how my whiskers had grown so long, and I also had to find out if I would ever get back to being visible again.

Don't get me wrong, being invisible does have its benefits, but I would really love to be able to talk and play with my siblings again and have them see me. And to do that, I must find the Orange Gecko. He would know how to change me back, but how do I find him? He kinda came out of nowhere, and then disappeared the same way.

OK, it was on the night of the fullest moon I had ever seen; it happened in the backyard, and Uncle Blackie had seen him, too, on account of he started his second life that very night. Maybe if I asked him he might have an idea of how I could talk to the gecko and help me figure out what I'm supposed to do.

It felt like it'd been a million weeks since I'd met with the Orange Gecko and gotten my new powers. I was lonely because I had nobody to talk to or play with. I mean, I did kinda like the time Uncle Blackie and I had spent together. I'd gotten to know him in a way I never had before, and we'd bonded. Even though I was invisible to everyone else, it was cool to be able to spend time with my only uncle, and I learned some neat-o things about him, and about me and my life. I still can't quite believe that I've been chosen. ME, Doody Newman, the brownest tabby in Texas, if you ask me. Actually, if you ask me, I don't really know much about anything anymore. I thought I knew it all; I thought I knew what I was gonna do with my life. I thought I had been living a good life, but maybe I had missed the point, until I'd met the Orange Gecko. I'd thought the best thing in life was getting a treat or a piece of cheese, but I can tell you now, there is so much more to my life than pleasing myself.

I was dozing off in the closet, when I heard Mini meowing in his low roar, the one he does when he's upset. He walked in and said he had to tell me something, a secret he'd never told anybody. Then he told me he could read my mind, without me ever opening my mouth.

I asked him what I was thinking about and he said, "You are wondering how your whiskers grew so long, and how to make it happen again."

*Wait—what? How did he do that?*

He then said, "The Orange Gecko told me it was the cheese. When you eat cheese, a few minutes later, your whiskers grow out like a million miles, and they have sticky stuff on them so they will stick to anything they touch."

*Oh, my good feline, how can he...? What the...?* Just then Mini got up, turned around, and started walking out. Before he left the closet, he said, "You're welcome."

I heard the big dog, Jack bark, bark, barking at something in the backyard, and when I sat
up, I saw a ton of drool on my pillow. *I must have
been dreaming... Phew, that was close, Mini with
mind reading abilities! I must be exhausted from
all this excitement. The cheese thing, though,* it
*does make sense. Think I'll go try it out.*

## Doody's Day Out

Iwas thinking about the day I'd gotten out of the yard. There was a hole in the fence, and well, I did what any curious cat would do...went over to check it out. I felt comfortable I wouldn't get into any trouble because nobody could see me, so I went out to explore. Then I slipped through the hole and started looking around. I saw the orange tabby-girl named Ginger at the playground. I'd met her last year when she'd sneaked into our house one cold winter night, after she'd gotten locked out of her house during her evening stroll. I also saw the jumping-dog from down the street; he was doing his daily rounds in the neighborhood. He sneaks out of the fence every day, and I'm sure his skin-parents don't know he is missing. Well, that day, when I

was outside of the fenced-in yard, I heard a lot of noisy kids laughing and yelling at the playground. I walked over to see what all the action was, but didn't feel scared because I was invisible, and nobody could hurt me if they couldn't see me.

When I got close to the kids, I noticed two groups of boys on the playground. On one side, was small boy named Clint, at least that's what his friends were calling him. On the other side was another larger boy called Cado, who was hanging with his friends. The small boy, Clint was crying for some reason. I went over to listen in on the conversation. He was talking to his friends in-between tears, saying the bully Cado had taken his favorite football. It was a special football; his father had given it to him before going to fight in a war in the Middle East. He said his father had bought it before he was sent away. They would toss the ball on the front lawn for hours the last few days before he left. His dad had made a promise to him that when he came home, they would toss the ball once again, and now he would never get to do that because the big bully named Cado had the ball in his hands. He was laughing and planned to deflate it with a pen. Well, that big bully was not going to ruin Clint's future plans with his dad, not when the brownest tabby in Texas was around.

I overheard him laughing with his friends and calling Clint a cry-baby and saying, "Ooh little cry-baby can't throw the ball anyway because he can't see through all his baby tears."

*What a mean kid, what a—oh yeah, this is right up my alley, haha. I am going to help this little boy! Now, what can I do—what am I saying? I can do ANYTHING I want, 'cause I'm invisible.*

I went to sit down, to think of what to do, and I noticed that the bully, Cado, was wearing brand new sneakers that had long laces. Ooohhh yeah, laces! They looked like my whiskers when they got all long and crazy! I had some cheese tucked in my cheek. I'd thought I would try out the thing Mini had told me about in my dream, so I had put some cheese in my mouth before I'd left the house. I maneuvered the cheese down the hatch and swallowed it. *I hope this is the thing that makes my whiskers grow. In the meantime, what else can I do?*

Hey, I noticed the bully's friends were hanging around the swings that were near the sliding board. *If I could get on top of the swing, I could maybe...* But just then, a dog came out of nowhere. Yikes, he scared me! *Good thing he can't see me! Maybe I can use his back as a jumping-off point, he is tall for a canine. Let me get over to him.* I jumped from the ground to the big dog's back, to the sliding board and then to the top of the swing.

I saw how the chain holding the swing was connected to the metal bar part of the swing set, so I lifted part of the chain link and removed it from the top.

The kid hit the cement with a "smack." It sounded like a deflated ball slamming into the pavement. He didn't get hurt, but was sure surprised, and it diverted everyone's attention to him. It scared him so badly that he started to cry, and he hid his head so nobody would see his tears. While he was on the ground, I felt a tickle on my cheek. *Alright, my whiskers were growing*! So, I wrapped one or two on the top of the swing set, then swooped down to the bully's friend who was crying.

I crept close to his ear and said, "Hey, you don't want anyone to see you cry, but you joined in when everyone was laughing at the boy whose ball your friend stole. If you can get the ball back to the boy, your tears will dry up. Nobody will know, and you will be doing something kind for someone else. If not, your tears will be shown for all to see, and you will become the bullied boy."

The kid looked around and because he had no clue where the idea had come from, decided to ignore it/me and got up to walk away from the swing. I could tell what he was thinking. *How could a voice come out of nowhere*? After a couple of steps, he fell on a rock sticking up, and it put a big gash on his knee. With blood dripping down his leg, he walked over to Cado, who pointed his finger, and started laughing so loudly it echoed all around the neighborhood. Cado walked away and started talking to the rest of his gang. The dog that had helped me jump, walked over to the boy and started licking his leg. Clint came over then, too, asked if he was OK, and gave the boy a tissue to stop the blood.

I swung over to Clint and whispered in his ear, "You know, this would be a great time to make a new friend; maybe he could help you to get your football back. Don't be afraid. He's scared, too. What if the both of you could join forces and get back your most treasured gift?"

Clint looked up like the voice had come from above. *Haha, this is fun!* He smiled at the boy and said, "Hi, I'm Clint," and the kid told him his name was Connor.

They started talking, and I turned to see what Cado had planned next. He was plotting another mean trick, and I needed to get in there to stop him.

My whiskers were working awesomely, and it was all kinda fun, if you ask me. I slinked over to where Cado and his friends were talking, and heard them say they were gonna deflate the beloved football—I needed to act fast. I got right in the middle of the circle they were in and looked at all the feet. Everyone had big sneakers on with lots of laces. Hmmm, I had a plan. *I'm gonna use all my whiskers at once to untie and re-tie all the shoes, and as I re-tie them, I will tie them all to the person next to them.* I put my whiskers to work, untying and retying, and when I was finished, their feet resembled a ball of yarn with laces and strings all over. I can't believe they hadn't noticed what I had done. Maybe I was getting really fast? I had to get them to scatter so all of them would fall on top of one another like a pile of bullies. I laughed at the image. Then I ran over to where the dog was and used my whiskers to tie his whiskers into a bow. He didn't see me, but started running in my direction because of my scent. As he was running, the bullies turned and tried to chase after the dog. As they attempted to run, they fell one by one, and rolled down the hill. Dirt flew, causing a storm of sand, which made it hard to see anything. When the dirt cloud cleared, and I could see again, I noticed a dark spot on the ground. *Oh, my good feline, it was...can it be?* Yes, it was the football the bullies wanted, only they had wound up down the hill, a ball of bullies, covered in mud, all tangled up together, looking like a giant chocolate-covered blob. Clint and his new friend, Connor, along with his faithful old friends ran over to the ball, scooped it up, and raced all the way home. I heard laughter in the distance as

I breathed a sigh of relief from the victory we had all just shared.

Well, my work there was done. Boy, had that felt good! It had all just worked out. In fact, everything seemed to be working out. Trusting the process and not worrying all the time really made a difference. Helping someone else kept me busy so I didn't think about the most important BROWNEST tabby in Texas. (I gotta be honest, I'm a full-time job; I'm all I think about, so lately this new action had me distracted). This doing the next right thing, especially for someone else gave me a sense of purpose I'd never felt before. I thought I would try out a little swinging action. Then I saw the light pole, and the stop sign, so, I schlapped my whiskers to the stop sign and started there.

I swung to the light pole, and then to the next and next. *Wow, the view from up so high was feline fantastic.* What a beautiful day it is was, not too hot. I didn't have a cat-care in the world. That gecko was right; he'd chosen the right feline because every time I'd helped someone who'd looked like they were in trouble, I felt better about myself and my new life. Who would have thought that the brownest tabby in Texas could be a crime fighter? I know it may not seem like the crime you see on TV, but I can see things that are a crime. Nobody should feel bad because someone else was mean to them, be upset because they are lost, made to feel like they are not good enough, or be forced to do something they don't wanna do, all because they are afraid to be laughed at. That's the real crime, and as long as the world is asking, I'm gonna help any way I can, if you ask me!

As I was swinging along, I noticed I could see into everyone's backyard. I saw those dogs that are always bark, bark, barking. They are louder than the big dog, Jack, and Jojo, the silky one, and Cooper, the bulldog, all put together! They were barking at what looked like a trembling squirrel in the corner. *I think I can swoop down and...* Whoa, all of a sudden, a buzzard—I think—came flying right into the path of my swooping. I almost crashed into him. He was broad with wings that went on forever. I got startled, so I decided to get closer to the ground. The air is no place for a feline to be, even if I am an exceptional one—the brownest, most graceful, whisker-swinging tabby in Texas—if you ask me.

I was swooping into that backyard with those big dogs who'd cornered the squirrel. He looked like he needed a little assistance, and I was just the cat to do it. I got all the way down to the top of the fence, and I was about to jump down and teach those big-mouth, bad-breathed canine barkers a little lesson in kindness, when out of nowhere, that buzzard came flying at me and threw me off balance, so I hit the fence and fell to the ground. I lifted my head, disoriented, scared. But when I looked at the buzzard, it wasn't a buzzard at all. It was, *oh my good feline, what was that?*

I was warm all over and a little dizzy. I hadn't seen it in a while, but it was without a doubt, not a buzzard, but in fact, my long-lost shadow. It wasn't the old shadow that I'd always had around me either. It was the weird one I'd only started to see lately, ever since the night before I met the Orange Gecko, and the fireflies, the night I'd floated in the rainbow.

I looked at him and asked, "What do you want? Can I help you with something?" And then we just kept staring at each other. Me, looking at him, him looking at me. He didn't say a word. I heard hissing, and I certainly didn't know what to think of that.

I said it again, "Hey you, whatever or whoever you are, what do you want? I noticed you lurking around, and frankly, you are getting under my brown fur, so can you please tell me what you want, or leave me alone?!"

More hissing.

I stood on my hind legs, although nobody noticed because I was still invisible. And speaking of that, *if I'm invisible, how can this shadow thing see me, and what is it? Whenever it's around, which has been a few times lately, I've gotten those goose bumps under my brown fur, and I've felt all weird inside, like butterflies are in my tummy having a party. OK, I'm on my hind legs, and it's kinda good nobody can see me, because my whiskers are just lying on the ground like a million kite strings. Boy, they are coming in handy lately, because I'm going places and doing things that this brown tabby has never done. No answer from the shadow, so I'm just gonna do what I came here to do and maybe that shadow will get the hint and leave. And maybe I can save the squirrel having a hard time with those loud-mouthed canine barkers, too.*

I took my whiskers and swung up onto the fence again, and as I was sweeping up, I used my brownest, tabby toes to trip the bigger dog so he fell into the smaller dog like dominos. Then I used my trusty whiskers to tie their tails together. That big dog had been right in the middle of a bark, and instead what came out of his mouth sounded like bar-eeeek. *Haha, that was fun!* The look on those dogs' faces was so silly; their eyes got huge, and the mouth on the bigger one gaped so wide I heard an echo coming from it. The squirrel took one look at the scene in front of him, canine à la mode, legs in the air, bobble eyes, and made his getaway as fast as he could.

He turned back one time, and whispered, "Thank you, whoever you are." Then he scampered.

*Well, that's two down. What other wrongs can I right? This was FUN. Now, where had that shadow thing gone?*

I decided to take a stroll around the beautiful lake right outside my favorite window, and it was the best, because I was finally on the outside of the window. As I was walking, I noticed a beautiful kitty. She looked a lot like Lil' girl, the Siamese-snow leopard blend with the bluest eyes I have ever seen. She was smelling all the flowers along the lake and had stopped a few times to lie on her back in the sun. This was such a perfect day in Texas. I wished all the days were like it. I was on top of the world; I'd saved that squirrel from those barking canines with bad breath, and I'd helped a little boy make a new friend, get his football back, and defeat the bullies on the playground! It doesn't get better than that. *Who knew that doing the right thing and helping someone other than myself could be so rewarding?*

I walked over to get a closer look, and as I did, saw that beautiful kitty admiring herself in the lake. She must have seen something she really liked, because she crept close to the water. *Hmmm, what was she looking at?* I heard her talking to her reflection—*what the feline?* Then, just like that, plop! She fell in, *or was she pulled in? Wow, I needed to get over there, and fast!* I started to run, but was stopped in my tracks by that jumping dog, who came out of nowhere. But I knew I was safe because he couldn't see me. Although I thought he could smell me. That wasn't a good thing. This guy was all over the place; jumping to the top of the fence half the day to see who was on the other side, roaming around town the other half. I had to get out of the situation because that crazy canine made me nervous. He couldn't stay still for a minute, and that made my nose twitch. I needed to get him off my tail so I could get over to that beauty who had just taken an unexpected fur-dive into the lake. She was gonna be upset because her hair had gotten messy. I know I hate it when I get mine wet. So, what could I do to get the nervous nelly off my tail? I'd seen a baby carriage pass by. If I could just get under it and catch a ride, I could make it close enough to jump off and rescue that Siamese beauty and be a hero once again.

*OK, here goes nothing.* Slinking toward the carriage, until *bingo—perfect landing!* I jumped onto the bar that connects the wheels, and the baby, who happened to be occupying the seat looked in my direction—*can he see me?* I think I heard that babies, kinda like the kitten I'd saved the other day, can sense or see things that older skin-moms or even fur-moms and dads can't see. So, as I was making my way under his legs, I winked, and I heard him giggle. I thought about how I would have looked if I were visible and giggled a little, too.

I rode for a few feet, and the closer I got to the place where that feline had taken an unexpected fur-soak, the more I noticed bubbles coming up from the very spot where she'd disappeared under the lake. *I had better get over there fast*, it had been at least 20 seconds since she had gone under. I finally got to the spot, and saw her paw prints in the sand. I did not want to get my fur wet, but at that moment, I was invisible, so I guess I didn't have any fur to soak. All those thoughts hit me as I was leaping in the air ready to do a nose-dive into the lake. My whiskers were still long, so I reached down to grab her. When I looked past her, into the depths, I saw a black area and what looked like hands pulling her further into the lake. *What was that*? I didn't have time to ask questions; I had to get busy. I finally grabbed her and lifted her out of the lake, but it wasn't easy. Whatever that dark area was, it was powerfully strong. As I was swimming toward the top of the water, I noticed that the beauty not only looked like Lil' Girl, she *was* Lil' Girl! *Oh, my good feline*, how had she gotten out? What was she doing down here? All I could hear was her speaking her native Thai language that she goes into every time she's scared or upset, and then she passed out. I studied her as I carried her to the shore, and started to feel sad and happy and scared all at once, but there was something else, too. I kinda didn't know what it was, or why, but I had a fluttery sensation in my stomach and not the scary kind, the nice kind. *Oh, my good feline,* I think I fell in love with her in-between the water and the shore. I laid her on the sand, gently moved her head to the side, opened her mouth, and pushed on her stomach. (I remembered seeing CPR on TV). It worked! She spit out the lake water and took a breath. Then she sat up and started crying.

I whispered in her ear, "You are OK. Nobody will hurt you now."

She looked around, wondering if she'd really heard something. I just cradled her again, and sh-lapped my whiskers onto the light-pole, and then, onto the next, and finally onto the fence attached to the home we all shared. I lowered her down into the backyard, and onto the soft grass behind the rose bush in the back corner that faced the spot where I'd met the Orange Gecko and the fireflies. *Oh, Lil' Girl, Azreal, why were you out of the yard? You must have snuck through the hole in the fence, too. I was so worried; you could have really been hurt.*

And then I whispered in her ear, "Don't ever leave the yard again. You are not an alley cat; you are an elegant feline who does not go swimming in the lake or roaming around town where you could get hurt. Please stay here, I love you."

She opened the bluest eyes I have ever seen and said with the softest voice I have ever heard, "I promise I will never leave again."

My heart was full.

# 12

## Doodikins

It felt like it had been years since all these changes had taken place, but really, it had only been a few weeks. I started to feel lonely. I saw my fur-mom and Prissy, along with all my other siblings, even the dogs, looking for me. They even seemed liked they were missing me. I would go about my day eating, grooming, sleeping, and trying to keep busy, but it wasn't fun anymore. I started to forget about all the good things I'd done, and I hadn't gone out to fight crime in a while. I started thinking about me again. All my thoughts went 'round and 'round and ended up nowhere. I felt sorry for myself. I was having a FPTPP (Feline Poor Tabby Pity-Party), and I would think of how alone I was and how nobody had seen me. I forgot the fantastic feeling I'd gotten every time I'd helped someone else. I didn't know how to get that feeling again, not when I really missed all my brothers and sisters, especially my fur-mom.

I heard my skin-mom calling me from the back and the front doors. She would get the flashlight out and go looking all around the outside the house. She even put up signs with my picture that read:

**HAVE YOU SEEN ME?**
My family misses me.
Please call!

But, of course, nobody had seen me because I couldn't even see myself.

I did have a little fun with Xander. While he was sleeping, I would move his toupee to the side so when he woke up it would be covering his eyes, and he didn't know how it had gotten like that. *Haha.* I also found the laser pointer my skin-mom had been looking for. It was under the bed in the master bedroom. Late at night when all the cats would get the crazies, I pointed it and everyone went nuts trying to get the red dot. Mini would start then Lil' Girl, and finally, Xander would fly in from the other room and knock everyone over. Until eventually they all scatted.

It got to be too much, and I went to have a talk with Uncle Blackie, to ask him if he had seen the Orange Gecko again, if it was possible for us to go find him? He said he had not, but maybe on the night of the fullest moon, we could go in the backyard where it had all taken place and call for him.

*Wow, that sounded like a great idea! When could we do it, when, when, when?* He said he thought the fullest moon would be in a few days, and we could try then. OK, but we had a plan and that was better than what I had, which was nothing. I was so glad I'd talked it over with him. It's so much better when I talk to someone I trust. When I hold it all in, my worries take on a life of their own, and I obsess. Alright, I'm gonna take a nap, and maybe when I get up it will be the fullest moon.

While I was sleeping, I kept hearing a buzzing noise, kinda like a bee or maybe a lawn mower or a leaf-blower thing-y, or maybe it was my skin-mom making something with that loud grindy thing in the kitchen. It got louder and louder, and I couldn't sleep. Plus, something was tickling my ear hairs; I thought it might be Rustaford, but how could it be him because he can't see me and I'm still missing according to him and the rest of the house? So, what could be buzzing and tickling my ear hairs? I opened my eyes, and couldn't believe what I saw! The fireflies, during the daylight, and INSIDE THE HOUSE! *What the feline was going on? Who, what, where, when, huh?* They were just hovering in one spot, and they didn't have their lights on. I didn't know they could do that, turn off their lights. Also, what I thought was strange was that they could see me, or at least it looked like they could. They were looking right at me. I opened my mouth to speak, and I got choked up like the time I had tried to talk to Uncle Blackie.

Then I heard in my mind *don't worry, you don't have to speak to us. We can read what you are thinking.*

*WOW! That was weird.* I thought I'd heard them say in my head that they could read what I was thinking, and then I heard or felt them say, *yes, that's right. You did hear us say that.*

*What in the feline?* I didn't understand. They then said, *Doody Newman, we are the fireflies that were with you the night you got your powers, and we have been with you ever since. You just haven't seen us because we didn't want to scare you.*

I thought back at them, *you mean you've been with me all the while, the whole time? You saw me help the kitten? You saw me talk to Uncle Blackie? You saw all the antics I've been up to since becoming invisible?*

They nodded their heads. *So, they had really heard me. Wait, was I dreaming?* I pinched myself and it hurt. I was awake.

I then thought, *so, how can you hear what I'm thinking?*

They said they used a type of telepathy called FFTFC (FireFly To Feline Communications.) Well, that was the craziest thing I had ever heard, or thought I'd heard. And then I was thinking, *if you ask me*—but they didn't have to ask me 'cause they already knew! I was so, so confused. They went on to say, in my head, that they had noticed I had been real sad, and that, except for the kitten I'd rescued, I'd been moping around pretty good. They didn't want to see me like that. They said they'd had a meeting with the Orange Gecko, who'd requested a sit down with me to discuss what he wanted from me and what was expected of me.

*Wow, he wanted a meeting with me? When? Where? For how long? How do I get in touch with him and how will I know when he wants to meet?*

*Oh, my good feline, what had I done to deserve all this?*

Maybe I have more powers, and maybe the Orange Gecko can tell me how to use them and explain some things that this brown tabby just can't get his whiskers around—when they're at the normal length. OK, now I am back to being the happiest brownest tabby in Texas, if you ask me.

I was stuck in my head, thinking about all my stuff. I kept thinking and talking and thinking and wondering. I felt rude for not talking to them, but they knew everything I was thinking anyway. It was a relief not to open my mouth to make noise. Speaking of opening my mouth, all this communicating by not communicating, by using the FFTFC had made me hungry. I heard my stomach, although it was a little loud in the room with all the buzzing the fireflies were doing with their wings. I do like those guys, though; they seem to be on my side and at the rate I'm going I can use all the friends I can get.

Then I remember that they mentioned, well they communicated or put the thought into my head, that the Orange Gecko wanted to have a meeting with me, *me*! I was scared, honored, and excited all at once. Every time I get scared and excited at the same time, I get this nervous twitch with my brown nose. It's not just any nose, it's the brownest nose in Texas (if you ask me.) When it twitches, it moves from side to side and up and down so much that it looks like I'm trying out a new dance or something. It's very distracting and embarrassing because everyone knows I do the "twitch" when I'm scared, and so it gives away my feeling.

The fireflies communicated to me that the Orange Gecko wanted to meet me on the next fullest moon, which would be in three days. *Oh, my good feline, I can't wait that long! I'm just gonna explode.* My whole life had been turned upside down, then right side up, then topsy-turvy, and 'round and 'round. I was so confused that I felt a little bit alone again. The fireflies communicated to me that I had nothing to fear, that I am never alone, and they are always watching over me. I just needed to trust the process. The gecko would know what was best for me and what my next move would be. I just needed to be patient and look to my Uncle Blackie for support and as a role model.

In the meantime, I would have a little fun teasing my siblings...

# Barkfest

I'm wondering if it's been three days yet. I went to talk to my Uncle Blackie about what day it is, and I'm so excited I can't even remember. *Now where could he be?* He has been sleeping in different places lately, since he started his second life. *What day did they tell me again?* I thought it was gonna be three days, so is it day two of three days or day one of the start of three days?

*Where could Uncle Blackie be? Nobody else can see me, so how am I gonna find out what day it is?* My nose had started to twitch, so it was probably good that nobody could see me. Well, since I couldn't find Uncle Blackie, I guess I'd have some fun. I was getting antsy waiting all this time for the meeting with the Orange Gecko.

I went outside in the heat. *Wow, it sure is hot in August in Houston.* It felt like a million dogs were breathing in my face as soon as I slipped through the cat door. You know that hot breath they have, very un-feline-like. And the smell, well, it doesn't smell like fish like Prissy's or Lil' Girl's does. They have the best smelling breath, like milk and fish and cheese all mixed together. Yummy... OK, so yeah, hot outside, like a million dogs breathing in my face after running across country. It's a good thing I got a feline follicle-trim for the summer, 'cause it gets really hot under here with the brownest fur in Texas, if you ask me. I saw the big dog, Jack, going crazy over something on the other side of the fence. I wondered what he could be all worked up over. Sometimes he just barks at nothing, just to bark. *Why do dogs bark anyway?* I noticed when one starts bark, bark, barking, they all start bark, bark, barking. *What is all that about?*

I mean, we cats don't start meowing and then everyone else who hears just says, "Hey, let's join in on the meowfest."

I felt embarrassed for him. So, the big dog, Jack, is barking something fierce, and then Jojo, the silky one, comes flying out the cat door with her black sleek fur trailing behind. *She is so shiny, I can almost see myself...if I could see myself.* She took one look at Jack and started barking, too, like she was asking him if it was a sing along and could she join? I think I saw them exchange winks? Then, as if there wasn't enough barking with the brown jumping dog down the lane, the black and tan shepherd around the corner, the red cattle dog on the left, the mixed breeds across the street, and the new guy in the house...Cooper, the bulldog youngster, made his entrance to the backyard barkathon by barking in-between Jack's and Jojo's barks. It became like one very long barrrrrkkkk.

*Jeez, guys, give these brownest tabby earhairs a break.* It's like they really don't know how unpleasant a bark sounds. Do they just go through life thinking the natural sound that comes from their vocal chords is music to anyone's ears? *Some canines can be so self-centered. Well, I'm gonna give them something to bark at.*

Since nobody could see me, I had to see what I could do to get anyone's attention. Maybe move something or make a noise or something. *Hmmm,* I was just about to slink my way to the back of the yard when Rustaford came flying out of nowhere and knocked Lil' Girl over. She screamed in Thai at him and ran to the back. This was all part of his master plan, to knock Lil' Girl over because when she screamed at him it made the dogs who were bark, bark, barking turn to look at her. He jumped on Cooper, the bulldog's back, then Jojo, the silky one's back, and finally onto the big dog, Jack, then into the tree, and over the fence. All I saw was a flash of orange fur go flying, pass the tree and zoom over the fence. The last thing I caught out of the corner of my eye was the white tip of his orange tail—it reminded me of a Creamsicle.

This got the dogs going even more, and they started bark, bark, barking so loud it made my ears feel like they were melting. *I gotta go inside*; not only was it so hot out there it felt like those million dogs breathing in my face, but it sounded like a million dogs breathing and barking at once. It got so loud my skin-mom started knocking her hand on the glass door and yelling out to the dogs to come inside. It was all too much chaos for this brown tabby. I had to take a nap.

I thought I was still dreaming when I heard my name called. It was a soft voice, and it sounded like my skin-mom! She was calling me, "Doody Newman, where are you? Doody-boy come on out. Doodikins, I miss you; please come home."

*I'm here. I'm over here, right here. I can smell your soft skin. Oh, skin-mommy, I miss you so much. I'm so lonely; I just want to curl up next to you when you are sleeping on the master bed, cover my eyes in the way you call "adorable," and fall asleep to your fingers petting in-between my ears. I love how you rub my brown ears; it tickles the hairs in there and puts me into a deep sleep.*

I felt something wet when I opened my eyes, and it was a tear. I was crying. I'd never done that before. *So, this was what a broken heart felt like.* I needed to have the meeting with the Orange Gecko, and fast. I didn't know how much more this brown tabby could take.

## Tonight

Did I ever mention how much I love cheese? I love cheese more than all the tuna with shrimp gravy I could eat, more than all the treats in the world, more than hanging out during the midnight crazies, more than catnip, more than those fake mice my skin-mom throws for us to chase, more than chasing geckos and frogs in the backyard, more than, more than... Well, let's just say I love cheese even more than I love cheese, if you ask me. I love when I go into the kitchen to that big, white thingy with the two doors on it that has all the food inside and meow, and my skin-mom opens the door and gets out a piece of cheese, folds it, and gives me a piece. She makes me get on my hind legs, grab it with my teeth, and gobble it down. The best thing about me loving cheese is that the only other cat in our house that likes cheese—well, he likes everything, so it doesn't really count—is Rustaford.

I was so tired from trying to find Uncle Blackie, being outside in the heat where it felt like a million dogs were breathing on me, and being sad that I was still invisible and not knowing what day it was and if I'd gotten any closer to the meeting date with the Orange Gecko, that I'd passed out in the master bedroom. It didn't matter where I slept anymore, since nobody could see me, so I lie down in-between Jojo, the silky one, and Cooper, the bulldog, who were next to the big dog, Jack, on the dog pillows next to the doors that lead to the backyard where all the magic happened that one night.

I think I zonked out because I was dreaming about cheese, about having all the cheese I could want, and being able to open the big white food-thingy with one paw while standing on my hind legs. I was licking the biggest piece of cheese when I started to smell something that did NOT smell like cheese. It smelled kinda like dirty feet, or maybe grass, or wet dog food, or old socks that had gotten stuck under the bed that nobody had noticed until they'd started to smell, or maybe it was... *Oh, my good feline!* I *was* dreaming. I was dreaming of licking a big piece of cheese, but when I woke up, I was licking the big dog, Jack's foot.

It wasn't the smell, but a noise that woke me, kinda like a "ppppfffttt," like a wind of some kind, and it came from under his tail. But it wasn't just the big dog, Jack making that sound; it was Jojo, the silky one, and Cooper, the bulldog, *and* the big dog, Jack, and all together they made a sound like short whispers of "pppffffttt." What I experienced next will stay with me forever. I looked around the room, and there was a green cloud of, of, of, dare I even say it?

As a feline, of course, we do not do such things, at least not in public, and if we do, they don't smell. And we *never* talk about it. But there was no denying it; it could not be anything else but a room filled with sleeping dogs' breath, and, and, Phfardts! *Oh, my good feline*, I made a gagging noise, and I had to get out of there as fast as I could, before I gave myself away. I ran for the door, but as soon as I was halfway across the room, I stopped micro-inches from Mini, who was making his rounds to his napping spot in the closet. I could feel his whiskers twitching, like he sensed something. I held my breath, not only from the smell in the room, but also so nobody would hear me. Not that it would matter because it hadn't mattered so far. He twitched his whiskers again and turned around and ran out of the room, and I ran behind him. That would go down in history as the worst smell in the state of Texas, in the United States, in the world...in the universe, if you ask me.

Then along came Uncle Blackie, walking in the hallway, like nothing was going on, like there was no crisis, like I wasn't missing, like there was no most important meeting in this brown tabby's life.

I said, "Hey Uncle Blackie, where have you been? I've been looking for you everywhere. Where did you go? I need you; I have nobody to talk to except the fireflies that came to me in the house, but they don't use their mouths to talk. They use this weird FFTFC thing. I don't know when the three days are up, since I can't really tell time, and I'm getting awful antsy about the meeting..."

Uncle Blackie sat down and cleaned his right paw from his elbow to the end of his toes, then stopped and licked his lips, and washed his ears, before pausing and looking at me to say, "Tonight."

# 15

## Xander

Mini Me and Xander have never gotten along and have had that ongoing fight, but Xander and I have never had any problems. I remember when he first came to the house; he told us all his story, (we all have one, but his was extra sad.) It was a freezing winter that year in Houston. I didn't remember that, but it already sounded like it was made up. He said he was not in a good place, as the humans that had him were mean to him and never had the time to take care of him. They rarely fed him, and when they did, it was leftover food from the fridge or stale, wet food that had been out for a long time. He got used to scrounging for crumbs on the floor, and planned on leaving the moment he got the chance. The chance came when he saw an open door one night, and he made a run for it.

He was so undernourished and underweight that he didn't have a lot of energy to run, but he used all he had. He ran, and ran, and ran, till he could run no more. He was cold, tired, and starving, so he stopped for the night under a car, where it was warm. He figured he would sleep, and when he felt stronger, would resume his journey. In the morning, he felt the car move, and when he tried to get out, got stuck. The car started rolling; he jumped onto the bumper and rode for a few feet, then slipped, fell, and skidded on the hard gravel of the road. All the skin from his paw-pads scraped off. He tumbled, rolled, and finally landed on his nose, which made a "crack" sound. He thought for sure he'd broken it. Xander crawled to the nearest gas station and propped himself up against one of the gas pumps, where he fell asleep. He would wake up every so often, as cars came in and filled up with gas and then left again.

The man who worked in the convenience store attached to the gas station came out and brought him a can of wet food and some water. He ate a bite or two, but not much more before the food was stolen by some mice walking by. They felt safe enough to get close, because by the looks of him, they knew he was not going to chase them. He said he doesn't remember how long he was there, or how many cars passed, but he remembers a really huge—I mean, he called it the biggest monster car or truck he had ever seen—pull up to get gas. He could barely open his eyes and hardly had any voice at all, but he remembers letting out a moan. The man in the monster car looked over to where the noise was coming from and gasped.

He walked over to him and said, "Hey buddy, you don't look so good, how would you like to come home with me and get better?"

He says the next thing he knew, he'd woken up in the front seat of the monster car.

The car was so warm, and he was so cold, that the heat was the best thing he had ever felt in his whole life.

Over the next few days, the man took him to that place with all the metal everywhere, where there are other cats in cages, dogs on leashes, and another man in a white coat, who looked at him and sent him home with all kinds of stuff to make him better. When he finally got the medicine he needed, he started to feel a lot less sick. His paw pads took a while to heal, and they had to be dipped in some cold liquid. He heard the doctor say his nose was broken and that there was a bad gash on his mouth that needed to heal.

He was in tough shape, but the man who rescued him stayed by his side and kept caring for him day after day, and night after night, until he could eat on his own. The malnutrition was so bad, his fur had fallen out on the top of his white head. He said that's why he wears a toupee. I remember when he showed up at our house. He was skinny and did have a funny-looking rug-thingy on his head. Eventually, Xander got all healed up and could run and play and mingle with the other cats. The man who rescued him was not able to keep him because he was always on the road or moving for his job. He did not know where his company was going to send him, but he told Xander he knew of the best house and the most loving family ever, that he was going to bring him to that house, and he would check on him from time to time.

He knew this place would be better than he could ever dream of. Xander went on to say, "And he was absolutely right."

I think he was right, too...and that is how Xander came to stay with us.

## Chaos, It's Time

I was sleeping and dreaming of cheese, but I kept waking up to see if it had gotten dark outside and if it was getting close to the time I had to meet the Orange Gecko. I knew when to go outside because the moon would be in a certain position in the sky, when I could see it through the windows that cover the whole wall in the living room. I was jolted awake by a noise that sounded familiar, and noticed it had gotten darker, but I couldn't see any moon. There were too many clouds in the sky, and I heard rumbling like it was gonna rain. I knew it had not started yet, because when it does, it pounds against the windows. The wind picked up, and the trees swayed from side to side so hard I thought they were gonna break.

The wind chimes went crazy, and that cat door was the busiest I had seen in a long time. Cats were flying in and out; dogs were running in, and then they would make a lap around the living room. They were running so fast, all I heard were dog nails on tile floors, like they were on a treadmill but getting nowhere. After the lap around the room, they would head outside again to race around the backyard.

I saw Prissy come in and dash back out again; Rustaford was close behind her, and Lil' Girl was yelling in Thai (I can never understand what she says when she gets scared because she only talks in Thai when she is in fly mode, and *oh, my good feline*, they were flying.) My fur-mom, Wig, was bouncing off the walls. That's how she got her name, by the way, whenever she isn't talk, talk, talking, she gets nervous and jumps at the slightest noise. When she gets extra upset and scared, she runs to a wall, jumps as high as she can, uses her hind legs to push off the highest point in the wall she can reach, and then starts running before her paws even touch the ground. It's funny to watch, but I can't tease her because I'll get the look. If y'all don't know what "the look" is, I'll fill you in, but some other time, because right then it was absolutely, without a doubt, the craziest, loudest, most chaotic room I had ever been in. *What the feline was going on?*

I was still in my cozy cat bed on the landing on the top of the stairs, when I turned to look down the stairs to see that big shadow charging right at me. I almost didn't get out of the way in time before Mini dove into the bed, and right behind him came Xander. I know, I know, they don't get along, but when there's an emergency or treats are being given out, they forget. Funny how that is. I'll have to ask them about it sometime, but right then, I had to get out of there!

So, I dove out of the soft cat bed and started to run up the stairs because that was the only place where there was no chaos. The downstairs was like a tornado, catnado, dognado. I ran and ran, and stopped at the top of the stairs because Uncle Blackie was looking down at the scene below from between the wood thingys. He was in his normal non-affected mode of just watching everyone else freak out. I sat next to him and watched, too. Everyone was acting so crazy. I knew not to ask too many questions because I would only get a one-word answer anyway. So, I just tried to relax even though my guts were spinning.

When I finally looked at Uncle Blackie, he said "It's time."

I swallowed, gulped down my fear, only to find it would creep up and scare me again. I was so nervous that my nose started twitching, and I started pacing back and forth. *When will we*

*talk? What will he tell me?* I had so many questions for the bright Orange Gecko. I didn't even know where to start. *What if I never became visible again? What if I can't do what I used to do? What if all my plans for the rest of my feline life are never gonna happen? Oh, my good feline, I'm a nervous chattering fur ball. I can't believe tonight is the night I'm gonna meet the Orange Gecko again, have all my questions answered, and then get back to my life again!*

I followed Uncle Blackie down the steps to the chaos on the first floor. I couldn't feel my brown tabby toes as we headed toward the cat door because I was so scared.

Then I stopped, and Uncle Blackie turned and asked me what was up. I told him, "Uncle Blackie, I'm so scared. What if I don't get to be visible again? What if the gecko gets mad at me? What if all this is just a master plan meant for another tabby and not me? What if whatever he asks me to do, I can't?"

He opened his mouth and what happened next, I will never forget for the rest of this brown tabby's life.

Uncle Blackie said, "Doody Newman, you were chosen to be the one; the Orange Gecko came to you and chose you. I know you think it was a mistake, but he believes in you, knows you can do whatever he asks of you, and knows you will not disappoint him. I believe in you. I've known you since you took your first breath, and I know that the Orange Gecko selected the right feline. I will be with you for every step. Whenever you lose your way or get scared, I will be here for you, always, and I love you."

Wow, I had never heard Uncle Blackie say more than a few words, and he especially, had never talked to me directly. Suddenly, I started to sense a warm feeling in the bottom of my tummy. It started there and traveled to my heart, and then my head.

I told him, "Well, if you will always be with me, I know I can do it."

He nodded his head, turned around, and walked through the cat door. I watched him disappear. As he led the way for me to follow him to the meeting with the Orange Gecko, the last thing I saw was the tuft of his black tail as it passed through to the other side and into the backyard. I thought for a second. *What if...?* But then an empty can of wet food fell on the floor and scared me to bits. I shot out the door without looking back.

## Meet the Gecko, Again

As soon as I'd flown through the cat door, I was thrown into a whirlwind of thunder and lightning, wind and trees, flower petals, debris and grass blowing around the yard, and hitting me in the face. My brown fur was ruffled so badly it was hard to see where I was going. The wind was so strong I had to grip the ground with my toes so I wouldn't blow away. I couldn't see Uncle Blackie because the wind was too intense. I got low to the ground and tried to make it to the back of the yard in the corner where it had all gone down during the last full moon. I was taking so long to walk to where I was supposed to go that I was afraid Uncle Blackie would leave and not wait for me. I almost hoped he would go, because my nerves were so bad I could feel my nose twitching. I couldn't hear anything because of the wind whistling in my ear hairs, and I couldn't see anything because of all the stuff whirling around the yard. It felt like forever ago that I had been sleeping on top of the landing where it was all warm and quiet. I wished I were there now. The courage I'd felt in the house just minutes ago, had started slipping away. *Where was Uncle Blackie? Where was the Orange Gecko? Where were the fireflies? Where was I, and where was I going?* I was just about to turn around to head back into the house because I gotta be honest, at that point this brown tabby was not really sure of anything anymore, but I did know a few things. There was food back in the house. All my siblings were in the house. The dogs were there. My fur-mom and my skin-mom were there, and I knew without a doubt, they loved me. Then...*what the feline?* The loudest crack I'd ever heard came from the sky, followed by a flash of bright light. And all of a sudden, everything stopped.

I thought I had my eyes closed because the light was so bright it blinded me, but then I saw a faint shadow in the light coming closer to me. I wanted to run even more, but was frozen with fear in the spot where I had stopped. The shadow got bigger and bigger, and as it got closer, I just knew it was him. He had waited for me. He had stayed, and he was here to answer all my questions. *Oh, my good feline, it's happening right here, right now.* All my cat days, nights, antics, and naps had brought me to this place, where my life had changed on the last full moon. I opened up my brown tabby mouth, and... Nothing. *Really? Not again.* I was getting bad at talking lately, and that seemed impossible. *Me? Can't talk? What the feline?* Then I heard those familiar voices in my head. I think it was the fireflies. *What was that called again? FFTFC.* I'd forgotten all about it. *That's right, I don't have to say a word.* Imagine that. But I didn't know how to act, and I'm not good at keeping my mouth shut. Well, I would have to learn quickly.

The fireflies in my head said, *Doody Newman, we are here with you now. The Orange Gecko has asked us to prepare you for your meeting.*

I said...well, I thought, *what do I need to do?*

*Just open your mind and your heart. Speak to him with love.*

*That doesn't sound so scary*, I thought. *I can do that.*

They left me with, *We believe in you; don't be afraid.*

I thought I was ready. But then he appeared in front of me, the bright Orange Gecko, looking much bigger than I'd imagined. He opened his mouth, and I heard music, like a harp or strings of some kind...organ music; I even heard mice singing.

He said, "Doody Newman, you have been chosen among all the felines here on earth, to carry the message to help people and animals all over the world with your kind heart and healing words. You will do many things for us, and as long as you trust the process, you will always hear the right thoughts and words in your heart, so you will never have to think of what to say. Be kind to everyone. Help those who ask for it. Right any wrong you can, and most importantly, forgive—even those who have harmed you or someone else. You have been chosen because of the light that shines so brightly within you. The love you display, we have not seen in a very long time. If you are willing to accept this gift, I promise for every good thing you do, for everyone you help, for every message you carry, you will feel a sense of love and gratitude in your heart that will grow and grow. This is the path that has been chosen for you."

I had so many things to ask, but somehow knew he would only be there for a few minutes. So, I just asked one question, "Will I ever be visible again?"

He looked at me like he'd heard me and said, "Yes, you will be visible again and seen by everyone. If you choose this path, you will be given the ability to decide if you want to be seen or not. You will decide how your appearance will best fit the task in front of you. Doody, you have the power. You always have. It is within you; look inside."

I looked down at myself to see what he meant, and when I turned back to him, he was gone. *What message*? I saw a faint rainbow. *A rainbow at night*? I was once again speechless. Then Uncle Blackie was there. He put his paw to his chest and stared at me with love in his eyes. At that moment, I knew I was the one. *Thank you, Orange Gecko. My life finally has meaning.*

I heard a thunder clap, opened my eyes and found myself in the master bedroom, on the bed. The thunder clap was Prissy pouncing on me while saying she'd heard a can of wet food opening and to "Come on!" *Uh, OK. Hadn't we already gone through this?*

I was about to jump down when she put her paw on my back and said, "Let's go, silly. We have a lot to talk about. I really missed you; where were you hiding? We've been looking everywhere for you."

Then she jumped down off the bed, and out the door she flew.

## Doody's Instructions

I told you about the first time the fireflies came to visit me. It was during the day when I was asleep on the master bed, and they told me they were there because I had been feeling sad. During the month I was invisible and after the second meeting with the Orange Gecko, they appeared to me again. I was sleeping on the landing just like last time, when they came to me in a dream. I was dreaming I was in the backyard calling for the Orange Gecko, when the fireflies showed up and used FFTFC to ask me if I was OK.

I wondered in my head, *how do I become invisible again?*

And they told me *you've had the power all along; the most important thing is to trust the pro-*

cess, to believe that you can do it. The rest is just a few words to learn.

I thought, *that sounds pretty easy, but are you sure I've always had the power?*

*It's not as easy as you think, Doody Newman. We are always watching you and we noticed you are your own worst enemy.*

I was shocked. *What are you guys talking about? I'm the happiest cat I know! I'm not an enemy to anyone.*

Then they explained, *you seem to doubt yourself. You live in a lot of fear. You worry about what other cats think of you, and when you don't believe you can do something, you fail before you even give it a chance.*

They seemed to know what they were communicating about. *How did they know all that?*

And then I heard, *years of experience, our brown feline.*

*I'll work on the confidence part and try to believe I can do it, but what do I need to say?* I thought back at them.

They paused for a moment, and I was so wound up I was afraid I was gonna jump out of my brownest tabby fur! *Pleeaase tell me, I can't stand another minute of not knowing!!!*

Then they said, *Doody Newman, if you think you are ready, you will need to be in a quiet place where you are sitting. In your mind, you will need* to breathe, and trust that it will happen. When you feel you are ready, say these words: 'The sky is blue above me, the ground is green below me, the breeze will calm this Doody, and now you see right through me.' Take another deep breath, and follow it with 'always there to guide me, please be sure to hide me.'

And how do I become visible again?

It's very important not to be fearful at any time while you are invisible, because when you do not trust the process and become afraid, you may become visible again. If you are trying to help someone, it can put you in a dangerous place. You, alone, control how well your gift can work. It's going to take some practice, but eventually, you will get used to your new life.

So, what do I do to get back to normal?

They replied, normal is a state of mind. Everyone has a different idea of what normal should be. So, remember, your normal may be very different than someone else's.

What do I have to do?

You must first find a blade of grass with dew on it.

What is dew?

Dew is the moisture you find in the morning or in the evening that appears on the grass and the leaves and everything that is outside. It's a gift, and is very special. It has healing qualities, and when used in the correct way, is extremely powerful.

I wanted to know so much more, but forced myself to listen.

*Once you have found a blade of grass and are ready to be seen again, you must sit quietly, eat the piece of grass with dew on it, and say these words 'I love my life, I'm grateful today, make me whole, make me stay.'*

*That's it? That's all I have to do?*

The last thing I heard was, *Doody Newman, you have been chosen. Use your gifts wisely, and remember to always trust the process, believe you can do it, and you will.*

I woke up to find the fireflies hovering over me. *Wow, they had communicated with me this whole time while I was sleeping. That's kinda cool, they sure don't waste any time.*

Then there was a commotion downstairs. I was hungry, and the timing was perfect. My skin-mom was in the kitchen opening up some wet food.

*I hope it's my favorite.*

124

# 19

## On an Airplane

So, I have to figure out first where I am, and how I got here, and then where I'm going and how to get back home. I think I have figured out that I'm in my skin-mom's suitcase, but how did I get here? Lemme think, I was sleeping, and I had that dream (the one where the fireflies came to me and told me how to become invisible and how to be seen again.) When I woke up, I saw them hovering over my head and then heard my skin-mom opening up a can of wet food.

As I'd walked downstairs, somebody tackled me. When I'd finally gotten to my feet, I saw it was Prissy. She said, "Tag, you're it!" *Oh, it was so great to be seen again! I love wrestling with my siblings!* She jumped up and started to run, but I saw some wet food gravy on the floor up ahead. She slid right into it and bumped into the kitchen cabinets. We both started laughing hard, because it looked so funny how she'd lost her balance and slid on her back with all four legs in the air. The look on her face was so funny, too: shock and disbelief.

After we could breathe again, we got something to eat on the cat buffet table. My skin-mom has been trying this new food out on us, and it is heavenly, almost like soup. I love, love, love gravy, and it's pretty much all gravy. I was so excited we'd gotten there first, because if my fur-mom had beat us, she would have licked up all the gravy. Both her and my Uncle Blackie. Well, we all sorta like the gravy, but her and my Uncle Blackie...they are such gravy lickers (we call them the GL's.) After we ate, we both went to nap in the closet in the master bedroom.

Prissy always gets first dibs on her spot, and she chose the round container that had all the fresh smelling clothes in it, so I looked around and noticed there was another container. It was long, not as tall, and there was a delicious smell coming from it. I didn't know at first, but I do now, it was my skin-mom's suitcase for work. She had clean clothes in there, which meant she was leaving for a trip.

*But wait, if Prissy and I were playing, how could I be invisible*? I had to have done something else after that.

*Wait!* *I remember.* I'd changed into my invisible self to go cattin' around while everyone had been taking their afternoon nap. I'd gone out back, said those words, and changed into my invisible self again. I'd only been outside for a few minutes because it was so hot that I turned around and came back in, but I must have been so tired that I'd forgotten to change back to my visible self!

*Oh, my good feline, I'm in a heap of trouble. So, that's how it happened, how I got myself in here; I fell asleep invisible, and my skin-mom did not see me and closed her suitcase for her trip. I was inside still sleeping. Here I am, most definitely on an airplane, with my skin-mom at work, in a closet-looking compartment on an airplane 35,000 feet above the earth.*

*I guess I'd better do some investigating; I may be here awhile. It's totally black. I can't see a thing. Even though I have night vision, which lets me see in the dark, I don't know about this place. I think it's like, double dark. Maybe I'm inside a suitcase that's inside something else. Lemme try to squeeze myself to one side... Oh OK, I feel a zipper, now what side is what? Lemme feel the length of the zipper with my trusty whiskers that have not failed me yet and that are still nice and long, thank goodness... Oohhh, here we go, I feel an opening. It must be on the top part of the suit-*

*case, because I always see her open that part to throw last-minute stuff in there.*

*I think I can slip out the top, or the side, the way it is laying. Here we go. Oh wow, I AM in an overhead compartment! There is another bag, and yummy, I smell food, like fried chicken or something. There's a backpack, pair of sneakers, and a light coming from another bag. I think it's a phone; somebody forgot to turn off their phone, and it's a good thing because it is lighting my way in this place.*

I looked to the right, and saw where the handle was to open up the overhead door. I needed to be really careful not to draw any attention to myself, because I don't think these people are ready for the likes of me yet! So, I used one whisker to open the handle, and another one to hold the door open, just enough to slip through it and out. I spotted an area on the top of the ceiling where I could latch on with another whisker to complete my escape from the overhead compartment. *Weeeee!* I grabbed on with one whisker to the spot on the ceiling and then kept going with my other whiskers, finding spots and clinging on. When I was done, I looked like a cat burglar, hanging upside down in the middle of an airplane in the middle of the sky. Not bad for the brownest tabby in Texas, now the brownest tabby hanging upside down from the biggest airplane I've ever seen at 35,000 feet off the ground.

I saw an open seat, so I swung over and landed on it. Then I climbed down and started slinking under the seats around everyone's feet. *There were some strange looking feet.* Some had fat toes; some toes were painted pretty; some toes looked like they had been mangled; some were smelly; some had socks. One looked like a hammerhead, *and this one over here, I think it has fungus? And...look at that one...with the extra toe.* Wow, those toes look like the big dog, Jack's. *How can that be...? Oh, my good feline, that's a big dog, and I think he can smell me. Yikes!* I didn't like the look of him; he seemed like he knew I was there. He's staring in my direction and growling... *I'd better get outta here!*

I turned to run but bumped into something. Upon further investigation, I saw it was a cat crate under a seat. Inside the crate was a small kitten, and he was crying loudly. I noticed then that I felt a little dizzy and stuff was moving around, like somebody was shaking the steering wheel of the airplane. I sat on the floor and tried to get my balance; *what was happening?* Lights flashed on the floor and on the seats, and I thought the lights were coming from the windows. Maybe it was lightning, like we have on the ground, but

I didn't hear any thunder. But then again, the airplane was moving around like it was caught *in* the thunder. I looked closely inside the crate, and as I did, the kitten who was crying peered right back at me. His mouth was open as wide as it could go and his cry was as loud as he could make it. I wondered if he could see me since I was still my invisible self.

I said, "Hi little guy, can you see me?"

He mewed out in-between sniffles, "What do you mean? Yes, sir, it's not that dark in here."

I was going to say, "You are right, it's not that dark," but instead fell over again. The lights came on once more, and the captain's voice sounded through the speaker saying we were going through some turbulence. *This is what turbulence feels like?*

I asked the kitten why he was crying, and he told me he was sad because he was going to a new home and that he missed all his brothers and sisters and his fur-mom. He said he was scared because he didn't know where he was and he had never been on an airplane, that he felt sick from all the shaking on the plane.

I introduced myself and asked his name. He told me it was "number three" because he had been the third one born out of six to his fur-mom. I told him he looked like a Daniel, because Daniel was a historical hero who was very brave and who had walked through his fear, to come out on the other side courageously. I had been told the story by my skin-mom when I'd been just a kitten myself. I tried to calm him down and told him it was my first time on an airplane, too. That I had been scared at first but I trusted all the people who were working on the plane (my skin-mom for one, and the pilots.) I also told him I'd woken up in that closet-looking thing attached to the ceiling and it was dark. He started laughing at my story, and it was kinda funny. He started looking like he felt better, and calmed down. We talked about where he'd lived for the first few months of his life and where I live, and about all my adopted brothers and sisters and how it's gonna be great where he is going and not to be sad. He will meet new cats, dogs, and people and shouldn't be scared. I told him that a wise animal had once told me that I should trust the process. That the process was some unexplained force that knows all my needs before I even do and will make sure it all works out no matter what. All I needed to do was be accountable for my own actions, and help anyone else who asked for it. Then the process would take care of the rest. I also said I had experienced the process firsthand, and I believed in it.

He finally said, "Thank you Doody Newman. The way you talk, you make me feel less scared, and I will try to remember what you have said. I will do my best to be more like you and look for the things that I am good at, and maybe I will have more confidence and people will start to like me because I like myself. I will try to help others and by doing so, will feel better about myself. I will start today and from now on, will call myself Daniel."

*Wow, that was extra cool. He saw me while I was invisible. I helped him to not feel so scared. I also explained the process and how helping others has helped me.* That made me feel good all over again. This new life of mine *was* awesome, but still I wonder how he saw me?

Suddenly, I felt a crash under my feet.

*What the feline was that? Oh no, I don't think we are flying anymore, which means we are on the ground, not in the air, and that means we've landed! Oh, my good feline!* I was on my back on the floor and I'd started to slide. I saw one, two, three pairs of feet, carry-on bags, a bottle of water, some cereal pieces, and peanuts. *Wheeee, this is fun, but wait! I am not in my skin-mom's suitcase!* It felt like we were about to come to a stop and that I would just have enough time to shoot my whiskers to the ceiling and swing. But as I was about to do that, one of those feet jerked, the owner sat up straight, and the guy attached to those feet kicked me and knocked me out cold.

While I was knocked out, I dreamed of that black shadow I'd remembered seeing a few times. I'm not sure what exactly it was, because it looked like me, but somehow, it was not me. I didn't feel it was a good thing, though, because I got a weird feeling in the pit of my stomach, kinda like when I know something bad is gonna happen. That shadow didn't feel right; even though it looked like a part of me. It still felt like it wasn't. It almost appeared like it had a life of its own, and I sensed it wanted to hurt me. I don't know why I felt like it was bad, I just did, and I am normally right about these things, even in my own dreams.

I woke up on the floor of the airplane, because feet were moving fast, walking in one direction, as if they were all going to the same place. I was dodging feet and weaving in and out of the aisle to swim upstream of the crowd. But I needed to get back into my skin-mom's suitcase, because if everyone was getting off the airplane, it meant my skin-mom would, too. And if I was not in her suitcase by the time she left, I would be stuck on this big tin can in whatever city it had landed. I had real problems, too, because my whiskers had gone back to normal, and I needed to find some cheese to make them come out again. Cheese has a substance on it that jump-starts my whisker superpowers and makes them sticky. It's kinda cool.

A lot of things were kinda cool lately, but what was not cool is that I was trying with all my might to get to that overhead closet in the back of the airplane and I was being kicked and knocked over. The people who belonged to the feet had no idea I was there. *Ooch, ouch, eech, oochie*! I needed to find some cheese and fast! I noticed a pile of crumbs up ahead. There was a trail of those crunchy, cheesy Cheetos things that leave orange stuff all over your whiskers. It's a good thing humans are kinda messy when they are on vacation, because that could totally help me out. I was walking toward the crumb pile, through the orange cheesy sand, and it looked funny when I turned around, because I saw my paw prints, *hee, hee.*

Then it got dark right in front of me. *What the feline was that*? I started to creep toward the darkness, but when I did, the darkness lifted. I couldn't stop what I was doing to figure it out because I needed to get to that overhead, but before I could, I had to get my whiskers to grow again. Then I thought I smelled cheese ahead! I ran for it, but right before I got to the mound, that darkness, the darkness I thought was just my imagination turned out to be...*what the...OH, MY GOOD FELINE...IT'S THE SHADOW,* and it was DEFINITELY NOT FOLLOWING my movements, it was coming TOWARDS ME! *How can it see me?*

I was still my invisible self, but that didn't matter, because it ran right up to me, and stopped a hair away from my face, so close I could feel it/ him breathing.

He opened what I think was his mouth and said, "Dooooody Newwwwwman, we meet again."

I said in the smallest voice, the same voice I had used on the table with Uncle Blackie, "Docar?"

I heard him breathing or hissing or floating or something, but whatever it was, it creeped me out so much that I got those goose bumps under my brown fur again. They were so big this time that it made it hard to breathe... And that's the last thing I remember before I passed out.

Cold. This time for real.

I woke up and it was all black. I couldn't see my paw in front of my whiskers, and I couldn't catch my breath, almost like I had a suffocating blanket on top of me. I opened my mouth to say something, and all that came out was a squeak. I tried again. My mouth opened with a squeak again. *What was wrong with me?* I'd never had such a hard time trying to talk. Maybe it was all the strange stuff that had happened to me in the last month. I didn't know how to take it, I didn't understand what was going on. I didn't know where I was and I didn't know what was on top of me. All I could think was maybe I was in the middle of that shadow. *Yeah, that's right.* Before

I'd passed out I remembered that shadow jumping in front of me when I'd tried to get the cheese and it had spoken to me. I had even answered it back, asking if it was Docar. Then I'd passed out. *Oh, my good feline*! I was inside Docar!

All I could hear was a loud hissing on top of the already loud hiss from the airplane, so it was like I couldn't hear anything at all and I was petrified.

Everything had been going my way, then suddenly, it had gotten bad so fast. I'd noticed when I get scared in my life, I have weird thoughts running around like a dryer in-between those brown tabby ears. My thoughts were scaring me more than the shadow or fog (or foag.) *It has to be Docar, and if it is, I'm in trouble. I need an escape, and fast.* I could still hear the shuffling feet above all the hissing, and that meant people were still in line to get off the airplane. If I were left on there, I'd be missing forever! What could I do? I couldn't see anything, and I couldn't hear much except hissing and feet scrambling. I had to think. I needed to go to my happy place and calm my nerves, because if my nose did the "twitch," I'd never get anything done. OK...slow my breathing... OK, I had to think of something calming.

I remembered Uncle Blackie's voice: *Doody Newman...I believe in you...I know that the Orange Gecko selected the right feline. I will be with* you for every step. *Whenever you lose your way or get scared, I will be here for you, always, and I love you.*

*Uncle Blackie*, I thought, *you are the coolest. Thank you for your wisdom and faith in me.*

Then, I felt a tickle from under my collar. It was one of the fireflies! He flew from under my collar and smiled.

He used his FFTFC and I heard, *Hi Doody, I saw you sleeping in the suitcase and was concerned that you may be in for an adventure that might require having fun if you'd gotten stuck, so I decided to come along for the ride. I hope you don't mind.*

*No way, I don't mind at all!*

*I noticed the Docar foag has been following you, waiting for his chance to change your good intentions to bad. Every time you get scared and don't trust the process, the Docar foag senses it and shows up to cause chaos and turmoil and to try to convert you to the dark side where nothing good happens. There is lots of drama there, and nobody cares about helping each other. They are selfish and mean in the dark side, and no light ever shines there. There is no hope.*

*Oh, my good feline, I didn't mean to doubt. I don't want to doubt.*

Then I heard, *it's OK, it's not too late. I'm glad I hitched a ride in your collar, and by the way, it's awesomely warm under there, and has that smell of the clothes in the suitcase. I can understand why you love it so much; the smell stays with you. We can do this together, with your invisibility and long whiskers, and my light and wings. We can figure out a solution and get you back into your skin-mom's suitcase so you can return home and see your brothers and sisters. You need to continue to fight crime in Texas. We need you. The Orange Gecko knew he had chosen the right kitty, and I agree with him. Now let's get a plan together.*

I was starting to feel good again, and the foag was lifting. *There's the cheese. I'm almost there, OK got it, mmm yumm mmm.* Just a few more minutes...*and wooo, there they are...* my whiskers!

I thought, *Mr. firefly...hey, by the way, what's your name?*

*You can call me Fred.*

*Cool. Hey, Fred! Jump under my collar and hang on!*

I schlapped my whiskers onto the ceiling and swung to the back of the airplane toward the overhead closet. All I needed to figure out was how to open the door and get into the suitcase without being noticed.

As we were swinging on the ceiling, I saw all kinds of people; short, tall, old, and young. I saw the baby kitten I had talked to earlier, and that there was a dark shadow over his crate his skin-dad was carrying. *Oh, my good feline, the Docar foag was following that kitten*. That was not gonna happen on my watch!

Fred communicated at that moment, *if we don't get into the suitcase, your skin-mom won't know we are here and we may get stuck without a ride home!*

But I thought, *I can't let the kitten's fear attract the likes of the Docar foag, not this early in his life.* And I felt responsible for Docar being there because of me and my fear, so I had to save him!

Then I heard, *I'm with you, what do you want to do?*

*I think we need to get rid of Docar, and I know how.*

I swung to the floor again, and once more, started to dodge feet until I'd reached the kitten in his crate.

I yelled to him, "Daniel, you can do this, don't be scared, believe in yourself, and trust the process. You are a very special kitty! You are courageous and brave and don't be afraid!"

His very small voice replied, "I'm so afraid, what if my new family doesn't like me, and sends me back? What if there are other kitties that are bigger and better and don't want to play with me? What if they laugh at me because my mom gave me up and I don't have anyone I know and what if I can't be myself? What will everyone think of me? It's all so scary I don't know what to do... MEOOOOOWWWW!"

I stopped and thought, *hmmm he sounds a lot like me. Did I sound that scared? Did I wonder all those things, and did I sound like a little kitten with no solution?*

And I heard, yes, *Doody Newman, you were like that very kitten you now hear crying, but you trusted the process, overcame the fear, and are doing better every day. You must continue to do the next right thing, and help other kitties and doggies and even people who ask for your help to keep that warm fuzzy feeling that happens when you are having a great day. You must always stay in the action, and the good days will come to you because of your hard work.*

I guessed Fred had said it all. So, I opened my mouth, and for the first time in a very long time, with a big voice I didn't recognize (I was full of confidence and love), said, "Not long ago, I was where you are right now, afraid and unsure and sad. I didn't know what my life was about. I had no confidence and no purpose. Something happened to me and then I changed, but this change came as a surprise, and I realized it was not something I wanted. I rejected the change and searched and searched for days to find what this change meant for my life, what my meaning was in life. It wasn't till this very moment that I realized my purpose is to help others to feel as good as I do by doing what I was taught to do. So, I share my story, tell others not to be afraid, encourage them with love, and let them know no matter what they will be OK. I had to do what I could and trust the process. If this brown tabby can do it, so can you. I believe in you, Daniel, and I can see you have that same light shining in your heart."

After I spoke those words, I felt warm all over and was almost overcome by tears. And then I was overjoyed to see the Docar foag lifting from the crate. I heard the little kitty say, "Doody Newman, you are right. I'm not gonna be afraid, I will believe in myself like you have believed in me today. I WILL be OK, and I promise to help someone else like you have helped me!"

Fred communicated, *nice work.*

*Fred*, I sent back at my firefly friend, *let's go home!*

I schlapped my whiskers to the ceiling and swung to the closet. Someone had opened it, so it was with ease we landed in that compartment and crept into the suitcase. *Aaahhh that smell,* yup that was my skin-mom's scent and I was going home. When I laid down, Fred got out from under my collar, and I heard some more communicating. *Who else is in here?*

*It's only me, Fritz, the other firefly.* Fritz went on to say, *I couldn't let y'all go without me. I saw what you did, Doody Newman, and I'm so proud of you both.*

I guessed I wasn't alone after all; in fact, I'd never be alone again. I was so glad that in just a short time I had learned so much from my new firefly friends, Uncle Blackie, and the Orange Gecko. It had all been exhausting and so I didn't fight it anymore, but went into a deep kitty sleep.

I woke up with a jolt to feel Prissy pouncing on me. I was still in the closet in my skin-mom's suitcase. "What the feline?" She said, "You were having some dream, Doody. Your legs were kicking and your whiskers were twitching something fierce. Your mouth, too, you kept opening it up like you were about to say something but nothing came out."

*Had I just dreamed the whole thing? Where were Fred and Fritz?* I told Prissy about the dream, and the foag and the kitten, and the whiskers, too...about it all. She started laughing. "Oh Doodles, really, invisible? You have such an imagination, maybe it was the fresh smell of the clothes that got in your head. Don't you think skin-mom would know if you were in her suitcase? Always looking for attention, that's why I love you. And hey, I just heard a can of wet food opening! Last one there gets to lick my leftovers!"

How could it be just a dream when I couldn't believe how real it felt? *Wow, I guess I am hungry*; all that dreaming had given me an appetite. I followed Prissy into the kitchen and onto the cat buffet table, and I heard Jack, Jojo, and Cooper, bark, bark, barking in the backyard. I saw Rustaford, Lil' Girl, Xander, and Mini Me making their way to the kitchen, too. I was just about to dive into some gravy when I sensed someone walking over. *Oh, my good feline, it was my fur-mom!* I'd missed her so much; I ran up to her and started licking her ears and her face and said, "Oh mom, I missed you so much, I love you! I promise I'll be the best son and brother I can be. I won't complain anymore and I'll be good, I promise."

She looked at me, laughed and said, "My Doody Newman, my favorite son, you must have had a bad dream again. You have such an imagination. I love you, too, and I can't wait to see those changes. But could you first explain why you left a trail of orange paw prints on the floor?"

I turned around and saw a trail of my very own paw prints in orange Cheetos. *What the... oh noooo...I'm not even...really?* Just then, Prissy finished, pounced on me, and said, "You're it!" Rustaford jumped in, followed by Lil' Girl, Xander, and Mini. In no time, we were a ball of arms, legs, whiskers, and ears. It felt like home again; but it was all going in slow motion. Somebody jumped out and hacked up a fur ball, and when I went to look at who it was, I noticed Uncle Blackie staring at me. I wanted to talk to him; I had to tell him so much. I had so many questions and wanted to tell him all about my airplane adventure. I needed to find out what he thought about it all, if he'd heard anything and what it all meant. But getting those answers could wait. It was as if he could read my mind, because true to his coolness, in typical Uncle Blackie fashion, he looked down, licked his right paw, cleaned his ears, then lifted his head back up and winked.

# Afterward

(Just one more thing I gotta get off my whiskers)

I kept thinking about what I'd heard, or thought I'd heard, while we were all wrestling around in that fur ball. Had I heard it for real, was I cooking up an imaginary story between my brown tabby ears, or had I really heard someone say what I thought they'd said? I hoped I was imagining it, because what they'd said couldn't be possible. It defied any sense of reason or what I believed to be true. So, if it did happen, if I'd truly read somebody's mind, I guess all the FF-TFC I've been doing with Fred and Fritz has paid off. It seemed like I had developed another power that I had no idea I could ever possess.

What I heard was, *Hey Doody, enjoy your little trip? You think you are the prince of the house. You always get what you want, and never have to work for anything. Well, I can't wait to see the look on your brown tabby face when I tell the whole world, well, at least the whole house, that I know where you have been and what you have been doing. In fact, I lent my paw in your disappearance when I zippered up the suitcase. Bet you didn't know that! I decided you needed to take a trip, a long trip, and the skin-mom express was departing soon. In fact, I saw the whole thing from the beginning, Orange Gecko and all, and this big secret you think you have been hiding comes out today! You think you got away with the great escape, but you can never really disappear, except when I make sure you are locked in a suitcase on your way out the door. I couldn't wait to see how our 'hero' would handle that!*

*Oh, my good feline, who was that? Who would say such a thing? Somebody else had seen what had happened? How come nobody had ever looked for me then?*

I started to walk off, then turned back slowly and studied everyone's face since they had detached from the whirling fur ball, searching for something, anything that would give me a clue.

When I finally looked away, I heard out loud, "It was me."

"It was me." ...What? Wait, huh? His voice, I knew that voice, even though it sounded a little stressed, a little different, a little, dare I even say, maniacally evil? I still knew that voice; it could only be him. I was about to say his name, but when I opened my mouth to shout it, the lights went out. The dramatic and sudden darkness startled me, and I struggled to regain my composure. Then as quickly as they'd gone out, the lights came back on again. (Okay, who was playing with the switch? And how had they gotten to it, when it's all the way up on the wall)? As soon as my sensitive feline eyes adjusted to the blinding light coming from above, I focused on who was standing before me.

He was so massive, I can only describe it as a giant wall of orange fur. He looked familiar, like a feline I knew and loved, but something was different. His fur was sticking straight out in all directions, as if he had been electrified, or maybe possessed. He actually looked like he'd used hairspray to make his fur stand out, resembling a lead singer from one of those 80's hair bands on those vinyl things my skin-mom listens to. His eyes had a yellow glow. This feline force opened his mouth, to reveal rows and rows of extra sharp teeth, and as he did, a charcoal-colored mist floated out of his throat with a hiss. *Hey, I know that mist, and that sound! It's the Docar foag!*

I shouted, "Docar!"

He answered, "Not anymore."

Goosebumps popped up under my brown fur from the voice that vibrated over my whiskers and into my ear hairs! I finally managed to reply and it sounded and felt like I was talking in slow motion. Like it wasn't me talking as I mouthed his name.

"M.I.N.I.?"

# Glossary

## (C)

**CANINE ALAMODE:** Dog pile up

**CAT BUFFET TABLE:** Table where there are yummy eats

**CATNADO:** Cat's bad weather

## (D)

**DEBONAIR:** High class

**DOCAR FOAG:** Evil shadow

**DOGNADO:** Dog's bad weather

# (F)

**FELINGLISH:** How cat's talk

**FUR MOM:** Doody's real mom

**FOAG:** Different kind of fog

**FFA:** Feline face ache

**FPTPP:** Feline poor tabby pity party

**FFTFC:** Fire fly to feline communication

**FAUX HAIR HAT:** Xander's gray toupe

**FELINE FOLLICLE TRIM:** Haircut

**FELINE FANTASTIC:** Feeling awesome

**FUR DIVE:** Nose first in the water

# (G)

**GEN POP:** The rest of the house

**GL'S:** Gravy lickers

# (L)

**LOOP DE LOOPS:** Fireflies do backflips

# (M)

**MEOWFEST:** Cats all meowing at same time

# (N)

**9 (NINE) LIVES:** Cat's life span

# (P)

**PHFARDTS:** Stinky smell under dog's tail

# (S)

**SCHLAPPED:** Whiskers latching on to things

**SCRAPPLE:** Lots of cat's wrestling

**SECOND STRING:** Cat that joins to relieve the scrappling cats

**SKIN MOM:** Human mommy

**SKIN MOM EXPRESS:** The suitcase mom carries to work

**SPIN YARNS:** Tell a story

**SUAVE:** Classy cats

**SUPERPOWERS:** Extra special powers that doody has

# (T)

**THE OC'S:** Original cats *(first cats rescued by skin mom& dad)*

**TWITCH:** Distracting nose movement

# (W)

**WHISKERS:** Hair follicles that come out of the side of a cats face

## About the Author

Barbra (Barbi) Ballinghoff McGee is an American Singer, Songwriter, Flight Attendant, animal rescuer and skin mom to all the Characters in Cattails. She is a world traveler and now a published author. Texas is a long way from Stone Harbor, a small town in southern New Jersey where she grew up. Show business surrounded her as a child raised in a multi-talented family, her father playing bass and singing in a band nightly, her mother, an actress, radio DJ, and stage mom to her brother who performed drums every summer on the Steel Pier in Atlantic City. It wasn't long before she joined her brother and began performing as well on the famous "Tony Grants Stars of Tomorrow" show at the young age of 4. It was no mistake that her first song was a lip sync to Sammy Davis Jr's "Talk to the Animals." She got her start in modeling after posing for a local photographer, who put her picture on a postcard that was sold on the boardwalk and in local stores, down the shore in Wildwood by the Sea NJ. Whether she was singing and dancing in school performances or acting in local radio or TV commercials, she knew without a doubt that she had a passion for the arts.

She studied Drama and Psychology at Mount Saint Mary College in Newberg, NY, then took a break to travel around Europe and the UK before moving back to the US to finish her Liberal Arts degree. In 1986 she started her career with the airlines in Newark, New Jersey. Working for the airlines has allowed her to travel all over the world, and sometimes twice. In 1991, she got a position at the Honolulu Hawaii base, where she spent 4 short years surrounded by the Aloha spirit. During that time, in 1993, she had the honor of being part of Hawaii Winter Baseball, as the head of "The Sharkettes," a group of ladies who served as public relations to the Honolulu Sharks Baseball team. In 1995, She finally settled down in the Lone Star state of Texas where she lives happy, joyous, and free today. She is an animal lover and describes that feeling of rescuing them as one of the most rewarding things someone can do. "To save a life and provide a home for an unwanted or discarded cat or dog who may be out of options, is the most incredible feeling, for them and for me." "It's more like they rescue me," she says, "because fur therapy is the best I've found." When she is not flying in airplanes or writing books, she shares her experience, strength, and hope weekly by carrying the message alongside an amazing group of ladies called the Miracle Angels.

Made in the USA
San Bernardino, CA
14 November 2017